BRIDGET IN WEREWOLF REHAB

Maura Byrne

ORIGINAL WRITING

ISBN: 978-1-908817-19-8

A cip catalogue for this book is available from the
National Library.

Published by Original Writing Ltd., Dublin, 2011.

Printed by Clondalkin Group, Clonshaugh, Dublin 17

Dedicated to Pat, Muireann and Ross

CONTENTS

1

A NEW LIFE

All around her, Bridget heard the other students inhale sharply. At last, the Principal had said what they all knew to be true - they really were a bunch of special needs teenagers.

The Principal continued talking, appearing not to notice the feeling of discomfort in the room, 'Here in Mallow, at Herr Wolf's international Institute, we have special programmes to help every one of you embrace your inner wolf. But before I talk about the daily schedule, I want to tell you about our teaching staff,' said the Principal waving at the nodding adults beside her and puffing out her chest. 'All of the teachers here are werewolves and with provocation, can shape shift at any time.'

Bridget eyed the teachers nervously: The men wore jackets with suede patches on the elbows, check shirts and corduroy trousers, the women wore pencil skirts with twin sets on top. Some of the women wore strong perfume but Bridget could still catch their pungent animal stench underneath and it made her stomach heave.

'We stay mostly in human form but some of us will phase during your daily shape shifting practice. As thirteen year old humans experience puberty so too will all of you. It's time to grow up and I assure you that in the next twelve weeks, we will turn every one of you into full-blooded who can make the smooth transition from human to woŀ.'

All the teachers clapped loudly, Bridget heard someone groan behind her and she turned around. A tall, lanky lad with a mullet sneered at her and muttered angrily in a London accent. 'One shape shift a day isn't enough for me, mate.'

I thought nobody here liked turning into a werewolf?

The Principal interrupted Bridget's thoughts again, 'of course, some of you have no problem being a werewolf.' She looked over Bridget's head at the boy who'd just spoken. 'And some of you have other problems.' The Principal moved her eyes along the rows of students, 'but rest assured, you will leave here feeling confident and loving your werewolf identity.'

The teachers clapped again. Bridget looked sideways. *I don't even want to be here.*

'And if any of you have plans to leave the school,' the Principal stared at Bridget as if she'd just read her mind, 'you can't. We have barking attendants patrolling every gate.'

Looking at Katy, the girl who'd introduced herself on the way in, Bridget mouthed, 'barking attendants,' but Katy just shrugged her shoulders in reply. The Principal saw this exchange and said, 'barking attendants are members of the Duhallow Hounds. They act as our security. Now before I introduce you to your teachers, I have one other matter to discuss with you,' the Principal cleared her throat and looked out the window. 'No doubt you smelled the wonderful odour from the river Blackwater outside. Besides the gloomy climate, the river is the main reason we set Herr Wolf's up in Mallow.'

Bridget looked over beyond the window hopelessly and sniffed. Even though the windows were closed, the stink made her gag.

Staring into their eyes intensely, the Principal continued, 'the smell has a very important purpose. 'It keeps our enemies away.'

Bridget shifted in her stance and looked around. What enemies was she talking about? Werewolves really only had one. She heard the London boy behind her snarl loudly.

'Yes, Eddie, your anger is now justified. There are *vampires* on the other side of the river.'

Involuntary growls escaped from all their mouths, including Bridget's, and for one moment, everyone in the room was united in animalistic emotion.

'Groups of incompetent vampires attend Dracul's College on the other side of the river. But don't worry. The river is full of garlic-flavoured cheese effluent that they hate and they can never cross over.'

Bridget couldn't believe it. Two shocks in one day. She was stuck in werewolf rehab with compulsory shape shifting AND there were vampires living five hundred metres away. Just wonderful!

The Principal introduced the teachers quickly and then picked up some papers from the podium. Looking directly at Bridget, she asked, 'Would you mind handing out the timetable, Bridget?' Bridget shuffled up to the front and the Principal gave her a condescending smile.

'Oh, and introduce yourselves while you're at it,' added Principal Goode.

Bridget turned nervously to Katy. 'Hi again. Where are you from?'

'I'm from Nashville, Tennessee, Bridget.'

Bridget was a little taken aback. 'My father was from Nashville,' she said quickly.

'For real? There ain't many werewolf families in Nashville. Maybe we're cousins. What was your Daddy's name?'

'Patrick Quarry,' said Bridget in a faltering voice. It still hurt to say it.

'I'm gonna ask my Momma later. She knows everyone in Nashville.'

Bridget looked away and noticed that the other students were introducing themselves. She walked over to the group and timidly nudged the timetables in front of them.

'Hi, I'm Andrew,' said the boy Bridget had noticed earlier pulling at the front of his trousers. He was still doing it but now he looked embarrassed.

'What's with the trouser grabbing?' asked Katy loudly.

Bridget immediately felt sorry for Andrew but the others laughed nervously.

Andrew reddened but then he smirked, 'I have out-of-control territory marking tendencies.'

A tall blond boy chuckled as he took a timetable from Bridget. 'I'm Roald from Amsterdam,' he said. The sight of his long tongue curling out from between his teeth made Bridget move back.

Behind him, a glossy-haired boy stretched out his hand. 'Thanks Bridget, my name is Dev. I'm from India and I'm allergic to fur.' Everyone responded with a giggle.

A sallow girl with stick-thin arms and short jet black hair introduced herself as Simonetta from Rome.

The Principal interrupted the chatter and pointed to her watch. 'Read your timetables quickly everyone. You can do the rest of the introductions later. Miss Joyce is waiting for you in the choir room.'

Bridget looked down at the timetable and gulped:

HERR WOLF'S INSTITUTE TIMETABLE	
9-10 am	**The Art of Growling and Howling**
10-11 am	**Shape Shifting Practice**
11-12 am	**The Claw Factor at the Nail and Hair Clinic**
12-1 pm	**Lunch**
1-2pm	**Lab Work**
2-3 pm	**Learning to Love Your Inner Wolf**
3-4 pm	**Dental, Oral and Body Hygiene**
4-5 pm	**Games –Pass the Weasel, Badger Hunt and Spot the Trap**
5-6 pm	**Dinner**

Bridget had never seen anything quite like this before. In regular school, there were classes for English and History but not here - every class had to do with being a werewolf. How would she cope with twelve long weeks of this?

Everyone seemed friendly enough but she didn't actually *want* to be a werewolf. Looking at the worried faces of the others, she realised that many felt exactly the same.

The Principal approached the group, 'there are other students in the school of course but the eight of you won't mix very much with them initially. However, once you're ready to move out of this deep rehab, you'll have classes with them. Come on everyone. Let's go to the Choir room.'

Bridget exhaled gently and walked out into the corridor. The smell was vomit-inducing and she looked around her, feeling more uneasy. Paw marks smudged every window pane, paintings of woodland scenes covered the walls and the song 'Moon River' played over the intercom. Bridget felt something sticking to her boots and looked down to see bits of straw peeking out from the soles of her feet. Katy skipped up to her and Bridget felt slightly relieved – at least she had one friend in this school for loser werewolves. But then Bridget couldn't help looking at the floors in disdain because drains ran along both sides of the corridor. She saw Andrew lift his leg up tentatively near a pillar.

'Stop that Andrew,' shouted the Principal from behind. 'You must not urinate in the corridor unless you're in wolf form. The toilet is back that way,' the Principal said pointing behind them. Andrew looked delighted with this information and rushed off.

'So the corridors are just one big toilet,' muttered Bridget, shuddering.

The Principal narrowed her eyes irritably. 'They are nothing of the sort, Bridget. A wolf might be caught short so it's necessary to have drains for when you're in animal form.'

Bridget felt annoyed with herself. She had already managed to get on the wrong side of the Principal and it was only the first day. Her shoe stubbed against something on the floor and she looked down to find a half-eaten bone.

The Principal cleared her throat. 'After class, can you tidy up those bones and put them in the bone cupboard under the stairs please. Enjoy choir and I'll see you all at ten.'

Just brilliant! Bone cupboards, open toilets and smelly corridors!

***

When Bridget walked into the Choir Room, the first thing she noticed was the enormous organ. Oversized beans bags lay scattered all over the floor and many of the students fell onto them, laughing. But Bridget stayed rooted to the spot, sniffing, not liking the strong smell of sweat one bit.

Miss Joyce looked at Bridget and sighed. 'We have anti-viral spray on the counter top there, Bridget. Just give your bean bag a squirt and let's get started.'

Bridget looked at the others. Eddie sneered and muttered, 'Weirdo,' just loud enough for her to hear. Katy's nose twitched and she looked over at Bridget. 'I don't mind the smell of animals so much but I hate the taste of meat.'

Miss Joyce raised her voice a little. 'Quiet everyone. I need to test your vocal abilities so let's start with Miguel.'

Bridget watched as Miguel who had thick black hair and enormous brown eyes took his place, tentative at first. When he opened his mouth though, only a hoarse whisper came out. *'Ghet your motor running, head out ... Sorry, Miss Yoyce,'* he said tearfully, 'but I lost my howl.' Then he looked around him, his face red with embarrassment.

Simonetta leaned over to Roald. 'What did he say he lost?'

Roald looked puzzled, 'I think he said he lost his owl.'

'His owl?' asked Simonetta perplexed, 'he had a pet owl?'

Eddie laughed hysterically, thumping his lap with his hands. Bridget looked at Simonetta sympathetically and she leaned over to her. 'It's not his owl, Simonetta. It's his howl... his voice,' Bridget explained.

'Oh, okay,' said Simonetta with a smirk.

Eddie teased callously, 'a wolf with no howl, ridiculous, mate.'

Miss Joyce ignored Eddie, reassuring Miguel instead. 'Don't worry. That's why you're here. Trust me, you'll be howling mad in no time.' She scanned her list, 'Saori, you're next.'

Bridget watched as a slender Asian girl named Saori bowed her head before everyone, scratching furiously behind her ears with her fingers. She opened her mouth into a delicate 'O' shape and sang. *'Get your moto'*

*runnin', head out on the highway, rooking for adventure
and whateva' comes your way.'*

Bridget tried to stop the giggles but when everyone
began to laugh, she had to give in.

'You'll have to work on not reversing the letters 'L' and
'R',' remarked Miss Joyce to Saori as she slinked back to
her bean bag.

A loud howling noise signalling the end of class broke
everyone's concentration. Bridget had a lump in her throat
because shape shifting was next. Andrew shoved Bridget
out of the way as he bolted out the door down the corridor
to the toilet.

'Shape shifting class is held down on the farm. Turn
right after the toilets and then follow the signs,' Miss Joyce
shouted after them.

'I'm gonna hate this,' Katy said to Bridget dolefully.

Bridget swallowed. 'Probably not as much as I will.'

Katy linked Bridget's arm and they walked outside.
Bridget's stomach lurched when the initial smell of the
river hit her nose. How was she ever going to get used to
this stench? Still, at least Katy was very friendly and the
others didn't seem so bad, well except for Eddie.

Bridget and Katy walked along a narrow path, the grass
flicking against Bridget's shoes. She looked across the fields
and saw flies hovering over piles of freshly heaped dung.
Grimacing, Bridget realised it was probably the teacher's
excrement. The fields were bordered by a forest and
pretty soon they came to an enormous barn, the size of
two football fields. Everyone else ran ahead of Bridget and

Katy. All Bridget could smell was wet fur. She moved inside the doors and saw lots of frightened-looking weasels and badgers. At once, the animals sensed the danger and began to screech with fright and Bridget felt so sorry for them.

The Principal came towards the students from the back of the barn. 'Alright, Mr Looney and I are here to watch you shape shift. We'll be demonstrating later for those with difficulties.'

'I don't need anyone to show me,' snapped Eddie. 'I shift all the time!'

Bridget was shocked. None of them had been shifting for more than a year. With a full moon once a month, surely he'd only done it twelve times. She'd only tried twice herself. How could Eddie be such an expert?

The Principal narrowed her eyes. 'Yes, Eddie. We know that shape shift practice may seem worthless to a hyper-wolf like you but there are others here who need to practice.'

'What's a hyper-wolf?' asked Bridget in astonishment.

The Principal eyed a very proud-looking Eddie. 'A hyper-wolf shifts too much. The animal side is out of balance with the human side. He is an out-of-control werewolf.'

'I'm not out of control,' Eddie shouted angrily.

'Watch your tone Eddie,' answered Principal Goode tetchily. 'A hyper-wolf is dangerous to werewolves everywhere. We'd don't want humans to find out that we really exist. Control of your animal side is essential.'

Bridget looked over at Katy and winced. She watched as Eddie slunk over to the side in a huff.

'Let's get started. Besides Eddie is there anybody else who enjoys shape shifting?'

Bridget looked around to see that only Roald and Andrew stuck their hands up. Only three of her class mates actually liked it. What a relief!

The Principal, tightly holding a folder in her hand, clenched her jaw and sucked a breath in through her teeth. 'Let's go down through the list. Bridget, your problem is?'

Bridget felt very self-conscious having to start the discussion and she lowered her head, whispering. 'I don't want to *be* a werewolf.'

'Not a good enough answer. There has to be a reason why. Your mother says your reluctance started *after* your father died.'

Bridget blushed and fidgeted with her hands. How could the Principal mention her father so casually, in front of all these strangers? Even though she didn't look at anyone, she heard audible breaths and sensed some sympathy from the group. 'I...I...don't know,' Bridget whispered.

The Principal looked away impatiently and fixed her gaze on Katy. 'I'm a vegetarian. I don't like turning into an animal because when I eat the raw meat, I feel sick to my belly afterwards.' Katy's sniffling voice began to break and Bridget put her hands out to rub her shoulders in comfort.

'I have no h-owl. I'm not safe if I can't howl at my enemies,' added Miguel.

'I'm addicted to junk food. I prefer a Big Mac and cola to raw rabbit,' said Simonetta screwing up her face.

Roald and Andrew chuckled. The Principal looked at Roald and smirked. 'Of course, a few of you have other little problems but we won't get into that now.'

The Principal looked at Dev and he began to sneeze. Then he wiped the nasal drip from his face and placed an inhaler under his left nostril and sniffed deeply. 'Mrs Principal, it is obvious why I don't like it. I'm allergic to fur. When I make the change, I sneeze and my eyes start streaming. I run into trees because I can't see where I'm going. It's so awful!'

Everyone started to laugh loudly and the Principal's eyes flashed. 'It's not a joking matter. You must all be proud of your werewolf heritage.' She seemed so intensely irritated by the conversation that she ignored Saori altogether. 'Okay, enough chat. Let's get to it. I'm going to strike Andrew and Roald.' Frowning over at Eddie, she said. 'I'm sure you don't need any help.'

Eddie vaulted from the rickety fence he'd been sitting on and as he approached, the weasels and badgers squealed violently. Bridget turned away and swallowed.

'Bridget, please turn around. I insist that you watch this!' shouted the Principal angrily.

Bridget felt helpless and began to tremble. Leaning slightly against Katy, Bridget fought to get her breathing back under control.

The Principal struck Roald hard on the head and Bridget watched anxiously as Roald dropped onto all fours and tossed his head from side to side, growling. His blue eyes changed to a florescent yellow and Bridget closed her eyes, digging her fingers into Katy's arm. The skin on Roald's back made a creaking sound as it began to stretch and crack. Drops of blood fell onto the hay in the barn and Bridget felt Katy's body shudder. 'I hate the blood,' she whispered.

Bridget glanced reassuringly at Katy until she heard the sound of ripping clothes. Roald's rib cage expanded and bones poked out from under his skin, as he moaned and thrashed about on the hay. His spine began to arch and lengthen and the muscles in his legs and arms started to pulse. Roald's body shook uncontrollably and he raised his head as his snout shot out of his face. Fangs and teeth grew quickly down, just as his neck extended and a tail grew from between his back legs.

'Oh no, not the fur,' shouted Dev hysterically.

'Oh, shut up you big girl's blouse,' said Eddie in a mocking voice.

Roald's new body sprouted millions of hairs then he dipped his head, quickly raised it again, flicking his long pink tongue out from between his teeth. Bridget felt utterly disgusted and her stomach threatened to explode. She couldn't watch another shape shift. She ran outside, ignoring the Principal's protestations. She heard footsteps following her and turned to see Katy.

Bridget's hands trembled uncontrollably. 'Oh Katy, I can't stand it,' she spluttered, 'how am I expected to watch this every day?'

Katy nodded and pulled her in close for a hug. 'It's okay, Bridget. I know just how you feel. We'll get through it together.'

Bridget looked at the open barn door and saw the Principal waiting.

'I can't go back in,' Bridget sobbed, running up the path. She was happy no one tried to stop her. She wasn't going to make it through the term. The last time she'd felt this helpless was when her Dad died.

2

HOWLO

Bridget woke early and stared at the unfamiliar ceiling fan, puzzled for a moment. Then she remembered where she was. The Institute. She shuddered and turned over in bed. Despite the fan, the smell in the room was a mix of musky and awful. She wasn't used to sharing a room. All night, she'd been woken by every unfamiliar snore and scratch. Katy, Saori and Simonetta slept curled up on their hay mattresses on the floor. Bridget had been given a clean normal bed because she found the smell of the dormitory so overpowering. She'd been told that it would be removed at the end of the week and then she'd have to sleep on the hay like everyone else. Bridget had no intention of making it to the end of the week.

Bridget slipped out of bed and tip-toed into the bathroom. The tiles were cold under her feet but she cheered up when she looked at the showers. Her shower at home dribbled water but here the showers were amazing. Steel rods ran from the floor to the ceiling with water holes at two inch intervals. Bridget stepped under the shower and turned the lever. The water pressure was so strong, it felt like a massage. Bridget groaned with pleasure as the large plastic bowl above her head deposited a dollop of pine-scented shampoo onto her hair. Taking a deep breath in, she sucked water up her nose and sneezed.

After Bridget stepped out of the water, she turned on one of the enormous hair dryers in the changing room. These dryers were specially made dryers for werewolves - six-foot high with three settings: human, mid-wolf and werewolf. She pressed the button for human and instantly felt calm as the warm air blasted her skin and dried her hair and body in seconds. In front of the mirror, she ran a comb through her caramel-coloured hair. Her mother always told her how pretty she was, with her grey eyes and lightly freckled skin. She had just finished dressing when she heard a loud beep.

Running back into the dormitory, Bridget quickly picked up her laptop. Katy and Simonetta stirred on the hay beds, and Saori mumbled. Bridget ran out into the corridor and sat in the deep, rather hairy, window seat, which was designed to take a full-grown werewolf. Her mother's photo popped up in her Skype window.

'Pidge, why haven't you returned any of my calls?'

Bridget scowled at her mother's concerned face. 'I've been busy.'

'So, how are you getting on?'

'*I hate it.*'

'You don't mean that, Pidge.'

Bridget felt her face redden. 'Yes, I do. You forced me to come here. I can't stay. I'll be home by the weekend, back in my own bed.'

'Now Bridget, you know you can't leave the Institute. You've only just arrived. It will get better once you settle in.'

'I'm not going to settle in. I want to go home.' The strength of Bridget's emotion surprised her, bringing unexpected tears. She looked up and down the corridor to make sure nobody was listening.

'Oh, darling, please don't cry. It breaks my heart that you're so upset. But there's no choice. Being a werewolf is your destiny.'

'I have to go to shape shifting practice every day. It's... it's sickening.'

'Give it time, darling... Have you made any friends yet?'

Bridget sniffled. 'I met a girl from Nashville called Katy.'

'Really?' Bridget's mother sounded slightly shocked and not entirely pleased.

'Oh course, I told her that I didn't know anyone from Nashville because Dad never brought us there.'

Bridget's mum hesitated. 'Who else have you met?'

Bridget sighed. 'A boy called Andrew from England, Roald from Holland...'

'Have you shown them your *Howlo* site?'

'No, not yet.' Bridget heard footsteps and looked up. Eddie! He was the last person she wanted listening to her conversation. Eddie sneered at Bridget as he passed and seemed pleased to see her reddened eyes. 'I've got to go Mum. I'll talk to you later.'

***

Back in the dormitory, the others were getting ready to go down for breakfast. 'How did you sleep, Bridget?'

asked Katy sweetly, wrapping her arms around Bridget's body.

'Okay,' Bridget replied. She didn't want to insult Katy by telling her that her snoring had kept her awake for most of the night.

Katy linked Bridget's arm as they walked together down the stairs. 'I wonder what we're having for breakfast. This place is so weird,' said Katy.

Bridget laughed and nodded. It did feel good to have a friend, someone who understood how disgusting this whole experience was.

'Don't worry about anything. I'll look after you,' said Katy softly. 'I just wish we didn't have to eat breakfast now.'

'You don't like porridge?' asked Bridget.

Katy raised her eyebrows. 'I heard Eddie say that it was a 'special' breakfast. I sure hope he was joking.'

Eddie raced past them into the small canteen filled with the sound of incessant squeaking. Bridget squinted when she saw the rows and rows of cages on the countertop. As she got closer to the noise, her stomach lurched. 'But it can't be...'

Katy swallowed hard. 'Well whadda you know, live breakfast!'

Bridget covered her mouth with her hand, her stomach threatening to revolt. 'Live mice! Surely they don't expect us to eat these every morning.'

Eddie rushed over to a cage with his name on it and opened the door. He pushed his hand in and grabbed two terrified mice, their little whiskers twitching as they struggled to get away. Eddie grinned and stuffed the mice greedily into his mouth. Bridget closed her eyes, hearing his teeth crunch on the tiny bones.

Roald, Andrew, Dev and Miguel came into the canteen. Roald and Andrew seemed happy enough at the prospect of a rodent breakfast but Dev sneezed and looked over sympathetically at Bridget.

'I can't eat the mice,' Bridget said. Tears pricked her eyes. 'I thought we only had to eat live things after we shape shifted.'

Katy read a small sign on the counter. 'Live breakfast is served once a week. It will help you develop a love of live meat whether you're in human or animal form.'

Simonetta's cage had a jar of hamburger relish beside it. Her poor mice would soon be covered in sauce. Ugh! Bridget looked away as Roald and the other males chomped on their breakfast. Eddie leered over at Bridget. A tiny tail wriggled from between his teeth. He had a live mouse in his mouth and was teasingly prolonging its life.

'Don't torture the poor mouse, just eat it,' Bridget shouted.

Eddie opened his mouth wide and Bridget saw the terrified mouse's eyes as Eddie snapped his mouth shut and began to chew. When Eddie chewed, the crunching sound reminded Bridget of crushing a beetle. She screwed her eyes shut and shivered.

'Bridget, you've got to eat your breakfast otherwise you'll get into trouble,' said Roald trying to coax her.

Bridget watched the mice scurrying about their cages, running all over each other trying to escape their fate. Feeling so sorry for the tiny creatures, Bridget opened the cage and scooped up two. Their twitching bodies felt so soft and furry against her skin and their tiny brown eyelashes fluttered when she stroked them with her thumbs. Her heart felt like it was melting.

Bridget ran out of the canteen to a small toilet, stood on the toilet seat, and released the two mice out the window. They fell out of her hand, landing on their backs on to the grass below. Then the mice turned themselves upright and raced off to freedom. In that moment, Bridget envied them so much.

Bridget washed her hands and went back into the canteen to find everyone had finished their breakfast and were locking their cages. Bridget came up behind Katy and saw, to her shock that some mice were missing. 'I thought you said you wouldn't eat any...'

Katy turned around and raised her index finger to her mouth. 'Shhh honey. You know I couldn't eat those poor critters. I let some of them go. I sure hope Eddie doesn't find them later.'

***

When they got to choir class, Eddie pushed Bridget rudely aside as he rushed out the door. 'And stay in detention until twelve!' Mrs. Joyce shouted after him.

'What happened to him?' Bridget asked Roald and Andrew who were lounging about in the big dog-basket style chairs – Andrew had his legs crossed, obviously wondering whether to make a run for the toilet.

Roald leaned towards her, his tongue extending out of his mouth as if he were about to lick her. 'Oh, he got annoyed because shape-shifting is cancelled. He wouldn't stop banging his desk with his hands. We have a double lab work class instead.'

'Yes!' Bridget stabbed the air and grinned at Katy feeling genuinely happy for the first time since she'd arrived.

On their way from choir to the lab, they met Eddie who was coming out of the Principal's office, carrying a small red book in his hand.

'What's that?' asked Bridget.

'That's my report card, mate,' said Eddie proudly, holding up the book. 'I just got a tick from the assistant Principal. Two more and I'll be expelled!'

Everyone gasped in shock, but Bridget was suddenly interested. There was a way out of this Institute after all. Perhaps if she could behave as badly as Eddie she would get sent home? But did she have it in her?

'Quickly!' shouted Mr Boyle, sticking his head out of the lab door.

The students filed into a wonderfully modern room with a dark wooden floor, full of glass cabinets displaying bottles of every colour and shape. Every bottle had a label. Some looked old and paw-marked, others appeared brand new. Rows of counter tops with bunson burners and glassware arranged in clusters had wooden high stools pushed underneath them. Bridget took a sniff. It was the only place (besides the shower room) that smelt good. The odour was of disinfectant, but it might as well have been roses to Bridget's twitching nose.

'Sit down!' roared Mr Boyle. Even in human form, his teeth were massive and his tongue was a vivid red. His bushy grey hair stuck up in clumps.

Katy tugged at Bridget's arm and they sat down on two benches beside each other, their knees almost touching. Eddie sat uncomfortably close on Bridget's other side. He kept peering over Bridget's shoulder at her laptop. Bridget closed the lid. Someone was scratching behind her. Bridget looked around to see a shy-looking Saori digging her nails into the skin behind her ears.

'A few fleas perhaps?' asked Mr Boyle, looking over. 'Maybe a bit of mange? Have you had this treated at all?' Saori nodded but Mr Boyle didn't seem satisfied. 'Do you mind if I have a look?'

Bridget cringed while Roald's tongue curled out from between his teeth and Andrew jigged on his stool.

'Mr Boyle, may I go to the toilet?' Andrew pleaded. Without waiting for an answer, Andrew raced towards the door.

Mr Boyle pulled back Saori's ears, examining them closely. 'Ah yes, I see you have some mite infestation and skin lesions. Do you have any fur loss?'

Saori nodded again, smiling gratefully. 'I have some anti-mange spray in the cabinet. I'll give it to you after class and you can apply it after your next shower.'

Bridget shuddered when she thought about live mites eating into Saori's skin. It was such a pain being an animal.

Mr Boyle walked back to the table. 'Let's begin. I want to talk to you today about many of the tinctures I've invented over the years. We'll start with canine parovirus and rabies.'

Bridget groaned and everyone followed her lead. She knew everything there was to know about these diseases because there were loads of forums and blogs covering rabies on *Howlo*. This was going to be a very boring lesson.

'Don't you have anything new?' asked Eddie rudely.

Mr Boyle raised his eyebrows. 'Actually I do have some terrific news.' He tapped his long fingers on the desk in front of him. 'I've invented a cure for leprechaunitis.'

Eddie burst out laughing. 'Leprechanitis? There's no such thing as leprechauns, mate.'

Mr Boyle looked astonished. 'You cannot be serious. A werewolf who doesn't believe in leprechauns?'

An uncertain, surprised titter ran around the classroom. Only the Irish werewolves seemed to believe in leprechauns.

Mr Boyle frowned. 'Pay attention now. There are lots of families of leprechauns living around Mallow and although we warn our students to be careful, sometimes someone falls asleep in a fairy field and gets bitten.'

'What happens when they bite?' asked Bridget, as everyone stopped laughing and leaned forward to hear more.

Saori scratched nervously. 'Do you think we'll see a leprechaun during the term?'

'I sincerely hope not,' said Mr Boyle. 'Once bitten, a wolf develops all the habits of leprechauns: dancing jigs, talking incoherently and following rainbows. A wolf can get so disoriented.' Mr Boyle's large grey eyes bulged a little from under his glasses. 'Anyhow, we now have an anti-leprechaunitis formula. So there is no longer any danger.'

What a dangerous place Mallow is; Vampires across the river and leprechauns roaming the fields. Bridget wondered what other nasty surprises were in store.

'What else have you invented?' asked Katy earnestly.

Rubbing his hands together, Mr Boyle wandered over to a large silver cabinet with a silver key in the lock. The students flinched – silver is very dangerous for werewolves – but Mr Boyle picked up a pair of yellow oven-gloves. 'Silver resistant,' he explained crisply, holding them up.

The students craned their necks to see inside. There were hundreds of bottles in the cabinet and Mr Boyle nimbly lifted up one. 'These are fade drops,' he said proudly. 'Every term, we have one student who can't get rid of their fur for a few days after the full moon. It's an annoying problem. These are powerful. Ingest one tiny drop,' Mr Boyle pinched his fingers together, 'and all the hair on your body vanishes entirely.'

Roald stuck up his hand and waved it enthusiastically. 'That's me. I'll need to use that, isn't that right?'

Mr Boyle gestured to them to come closer and everyone rushed over and formed a circle around him. Bridget felt

Roald close to her and she turned to look at him. His tongue was hanging out again and it was covered in a white fungus-like coating. She frowned and looked quickly away.

Mr Boyle lowered his voice. 'A word of warning. These fade drops are very dangerous. Only I am authorised to use them, is that clear?' His voice had become stern. 'That's why we have a silver key with special gloves. If you drink a little, you can fade away for a while – but drink too much and you will never be seen again.'

Bridget suddenly felt excited. Perhaps if she drank some of these fade drops, she could disappear from the barking attendants' view and run away home!

Mr Boyle replaced the bottle in the cabinet and took out a flat emerald green tin. 'That's grazing salve. You will get cuts and wounds from time to time and this will repair your skin quickly. I've invented an accelerated healing ointment too. It's splendid.' He reached further into the cabinet. 'Saori, here's the mange-mix. I'll distil it into a smaller container and leave it for you at the next class.'

Saori thanked him shyly with a bowed head and clasped hands. 'We've got remedies for myxomatosis, distemper, bovine tuberculosis, Lyme disease. You name it, we've got the cure in this cabinet.'

'What's that?' asked Katy, pointing to a small violet-coloured bottle, shaped like a garlic bulb.

'That's none of your business,' said Mr Boyle curtly and he slammed the door shut quickly.

Bridget and Katy looked at each other in surprise. 'Now I'm interested,' said Bridget under her breath.

When it was time to go to the farm for lunch, Bridget's stomach turned over. She hung back as Eddie, Roald, Andrew, Dev, Miguel, Saori and Simonetta scampered down the woodland path. The distant screeching of the weasels made her grit her teeth and she sat down determinedly on the grass under the trees.

'Aren't you going to go in the barn?' asked Katy nervously. 'What are you going to have for lunch?'

'I asked the cook in the kitchen for a cheese breakfast roll instead.' Bridget gently unwrapped the tinfoil packet. 'Do you want some?'

'Is it mouldy cheese?'

'Oh no, of course not – it's pre-mouldy. Totally fresh.'

'Ooh, delicious.' Yet Katy didn't sound that keen. Bridget was almost going to comment on it, but then Katy took half the sandwich from her and devoured it in one bite. She must have liked it after all.

Roald and Eddie came out of the barn first. Blood covered Roald's torn shirt and trousers and his tongue looked like it had stretched down to his belly button. 'Lovely lunch, isn't it?' he said grinning at Bridget. 'Won't you join us?'

Bridget shuddered. 'No. And don't come near me. I don't want blood on my blouse.'

Eddie laughed. 'You're such a freak.'

Bridget felt her frustration rise but as she was about to stand up, Katy tugged her arm. 'He ain't worth it, Bridget. Just ignore him.'

Dev had a go at Eddie. 'Bridget doesn't like it. Can't you leave her alone, Eddie?'

'Shut up, you disgusting snot bag!' Eddie shouted back.

Bridget jumped up and ran back up the field. Hateful Eddie, hateful place.

When she got inside, she raced up the corridor. The lab door was slightly open and as she passed it, she slowed to a walk. Inside, she saw Mr Boyle bending down, the yellow gloves in his hands. Bridget stood out of sight, peeping though the crack of the door, holding her breath. Mr Boyle opened a tiny door in the skirting board and slipped the gloves inside. Bridget's heart felt like it would burst out of her chest. She tip-toed away, then ran up to her dormitory, delighted with her discovery.

That evening, the Principal came into the students' common room. She was unusually friendly and everyone stopped talking and got to their feet. 'Good evening all. I apologise that I wasn't here for shape shifting today but rest assured I will be here tomorrow. Meanwhile, there are a couple of things that I want to discuss with you. I expect everyone will be delighted except possibly Bridget and Katy.'

The Principal smiled but Bridget's pulse raced and she had a nagging feeling in the pit of her stomach. Had she been spotted spying on Mr Boyle?

'At Halloween, our annual lupine festival, we will visit Mallow Castle. It has a stock of three hundred deer, and there will be a magnificent live hunt and feast.'

A groan of pleasure broke from the group. Bridget looked over at Katy, whose eyes were shining. When she saw Bridget looking at her, she scowled at the horror of eating live deer.

'That's one of the things we'll be doing on Halloween night,' continued the Principal. 'And if we see you making progress in your lessons, we'll consider holding a party. And here's something I know Bridget will like – before we go to hunt at the castle, we'll be visiting the emotional roller coaster.'

Bridget's stomach flipped and she felt her head throb. Her mother must have been talking to the Principal because only her mother knew how much Bridget had always wanted to ride on the emotional roller coaster. But why was the Principal suddenly so keen to keep Bridget happy? Maybe Bridget's mother had told the Principal about Bridget's plan to run away.

The Principal raised her voice to be heard above the whooping. 'Bridget will tell you about the emotional roller coaster in a minute. That's after she's shown you *Howlo,* the impressive werewolf networking website she set up.'

Bridget was surprised at the sudden attention the Principal was giving her. She hadn't had time to go on *Howlo* for two whole days and now the Principal was suggesting that she show everyone the site.

'All right, I'll let you get on with it. Lights out at ten,' said the Principal, walking off. Everyone was staring admiringly at Bridget; only Eddie seemed to be unimpressed.

'Can we look at your site now?' asked Katy excitedly.

'Yeah, sure.' Bridget tried to sound nonchalant as she opened her laptop and the students crowded around her.

Bridget clicked on the *Howlo* button, and rows of thumbnail images were suddenly displayed. Each image was a pair of photographs, a human face and a wolf face, and all were arranged in alphabetical order.

'How many members have you got?' asked Katy.

'Up to last weekend, eight thousand, four hundred and one.'

'Amazing! And you created all this on your own?' asked Roald, his eyes widening.

'Well my Dad helped me... before he died.' Bridget felt a sudden pang of loneliness.

'Sorry to hear about that.' Andrew's tone was gentle. But as Bridget's eyes started to well up, he changed the subject. 'Can you find members by location?'

'Yep. Are you trying to find someone?' Bridget swallowed the lump in her throat, and put thoughts of her father out of her head.

'Can you look up Oxford?'

Bridget typed 'Oxford' into her search engine, and a long list of names appeared on the screen. Andrew scanned the names, and cried out in delight. 'Yes, I can see two friends of mine there! That's amazing."

'Can I look up Nashville?' asked Katy. Bridget moved to one side to allow Katy to type. In an instant, Katy brought up a profile and she began to scream. 'It's my school friend, Helen.'

Bridget bounced in her seat with excitement. 'Helen emails me every single day. I can't believe you know her too! What's she like?'

Katy squeezed Bridget's arm, 'Helen's awesome. She goes horse riding with me every Sunday. Hey, I've got an idea, why don't we all upload our profiles tonight?'

'What a brilliant idea! I can help you all with it, if you like.' Bridget dug her hands into her cardigan pocket. 'Andrew, here's my camera – would you mind taking a photo of everyone, please? I can upload all the images and attach them to each of your profiles.'

Eddie moved in beside Bridget and she tried to stop herself shivering as she felt his hot breath on her face. 'You able to find any members who are Chelsea football fans?'

Bridget wasn't sure she wanted to help Eddie, but her natural enthusiasm for *Howlo* made her ignore what a creep he was. 'Yes, there's a hobby search engine.' She typed in the words Chelsea Football and an amazingly huge list of names appeared on the screen.

'I did try-outs for Chelsea a couple of months ago. I'm a massive fan,' Eddie said as he nudged Bridget out of the way and took the keyboard in his hands.

Bridget watched happily as everyone rushed about taking photos. The girls posed endlessly, finding fault with every photo. Bridget uploaded everyone's profile slowly, checking that they were happy with their information. The school computers had two keyboards – the normal one used by the students in human form and an oversized, extremely dirty one for when they were wolves.

Later, when they were sitting around drinking frothy hot chocolate and chatting about *Howlo*, Katy asked. 'So, now can you tell us about the emotional roller coaster?'

Bridget grinned. 'I've always wanted to go on one but my Mum would never let me. It's brilliant. You get on this rollercoaster and you feel every emotion possible – joy, sadness, guilt, jealousy, anger and vulnerability... just everything imaginable. There are at least thirty-eight mood-swings included in the ride. You fly from left to right feeling all these different emotions. Apparently, it's thrilling and terrifying and so much fun. I can't believe we're going.'

Roald snorted with amazement. 'Unbelievable. How can such a thing exist?'

'Awesome, truly awesome,' drawled Katy.

For the first time since she'd arrived at the Institute, Bridget was totally relaxed. Then she remembered tomorrow's shape shift and she stiffened up again. If only she could get through two more weeks of rehab. She thought about the cabinet in the lab - maybe she'd find some answers there. She'd have to think of something to get her through because she desperately wanted that ride on the emotional roller coaster.

3

BRIDGET'S FIRST SHAPE SHIFT

Bridget and Katy chuckled when they heard Roald and Andrew. 'I promised the Principal that I wouldn't let you pee in the corridor,' said Roald, tugging at Andrew's sleeve. Andrew reddened and rushed off when he saw Bridget and Katy.

Bridget couldn't help but admire Road's kind nature. He was always looking out for Andrew, making sure that he didn't get into trouble. 'You're a good friend,' said Bridget to Roald patting him on the arm. Roald turned around and gave Bridget a massive lick.

When Bridget felt the furry substance on the top of his tongue make contact with her face, she stopped dead and spluttered. 'Oh, my goodness, don't ever do that again!' she said wiping her face furiously. Roald's grin faded and Bridget realised that she had hurt his feelings. 'Oh, I'm...so sorry. I didn't mean to offend you. It's just that -.'

'I know,' said Roald, his smile returning and his tongue still hanging out.

'Who's that?' shouted Katy suddenly, pointing.

Bridget looked out the window and laughed out loud. 'Oh that's Paddy the Painter. Come on, I'll introduce you.'

Everyone rushed outside to see a large werewolf standing on his hind legs, painting the wall. There was nothing especially remarkable about seeing a werewolf or even seeing a werewolf painting but Paddy was no normal werewolf painter: Paddy was using not one, but *four* brushes all at once.

'Oh my, I've never seen anything like this,' said Katy.

Everyone watched as Paddy held a brush in each of his front paws. In addition, he gripped one brush in his mouth and one in his tail. Paddy had patented it the 'Four-Brush Technique.' Developing the muscles of his tail to hold a paint brush had taken years to master. Of course, it was a little messy when all four brushes were moving at speed down a wall, so to avoid splatters, Paddy had surrounded himself with huge dust sheets which lay crumpled on the ground.

'Paddy, how are you?' shouted Bridget as they approached him.

Paddy stopped mid-hum and turned around. His huge mouth grinned when he saw Bridget. He clenched his teeth to steady his brush and mumbled, 'Oh, hi ya Pidge. Your mother told me to look out for you. How're you getting on?'

Bridget was irritated that he'd called her by her nickname. 'Hope you won't be spying on me Paddy,' she said as she quickly introduced him to all her friends.

As they walked off, Bridget warned. 'Don't get caught up in too many conversations with Paddy. He's one of those Irish werewolves who always answers a question with a question. He could keep you there for hours.'

***

The Principal stood in front of Bridget and raised her hand. 'I'll hit you once,' she said in a commanding voice.

Bridget trembled, hating what was about to happen but knowing that there was no way out now. Not only was she expected to metamorphose but she had to do it in front of the others. She knew the embarrassment was written all over her cowering body.

***

'Come on,' provoked the Principal. 'I've got your father's file in my office. And you're just as immature as he was. You need to grow up and accept your destiny.'

Bridget felt the anger in her chest, her head, her temples. How dare the Principal say anything bad about Dad! And what did she mean that Bridget was just like him, not ready to grow up? Feeling a blow to her head, Bridget's eyes flashed in rage. The Principal panted and took a step back. Bridget's vision became blurry for an instant and her mouth tasted of metal. The saliva swirled inside it and she sniffed deeply.

Incoherent jeering peppered the background and her ears pricked up – it was Eddie's voice. Turning her head and glaring at him made his mouth stop moving. As Bridget's hearing became stronger, the other voices in the room became louder and more distinctive, her vision sharpened.

Bridget fell on all fours as the sharpest pain she'd ever felt racked her body. Her heart pounded in her chest, the pressure building up in her body, right before her neck and ribcage expanded. Looking down, the enlarging ribs jutted out of her skin and she growled. Bridget writhed around on the hay growling and howling in agony as she felt her skin stretching and stretching, impossibly taut. She howled again as her hands and feet extended into long paws with large claws on each end.

Bridget's snout formed and long canines grew down and touched her tongue which she then flicked between her teeth. Shaking her body, Bridget's clothes fell onto the hay. She twisted her body around and felt tickled by the hair that grew all over. Stretching out her back and then her front legs, her back arched magnificently. The sound of squealing made her stomach grumble and she ran her tongue along her teeth. Two weasels were screaming in the corner. Bridget was an animal now and she needed to feed.

***

'You did very well particularly since this was your first time to do it fully,' said the Principal sounding very satisfied.

Bridget shivered. She'd just stopped vomiting on the hay and the combined smell of blood, guts and vomit was making her stomach convulse again. Looking around, she saw a fresh set of clothes and grabbed them. She was glad the ordeal was over.

The Principal came closer to the screen behind where Bridget was dressing herself and Bridget pressed a blouse against her chest. Only one thing was important now, showering this horrible muck off her body as soon as possible.

As Principal Goode continued talking, the smugness in her voice irritated Bridget. 'Of course, there were one or two small problems, but we'll work on that.'

When Bridget came out from behind the screen, everyone clapped loudly. Katy rushed forward and hugged her. 'You did real good, darling.'

'Except for the tail,' taunted Eddie.

'What does he mean?' Bridget mumbled, looking at the Principal.

The Principal gave Eddie a dirty look and said. 'Well, your tail didn't develop but that's okay. How do you feel?'

'Wretched. And I stink.'

'Get used to it,' guffawed Roald.

Katy continued to hug Bridget closely. 'You sure loved eating the meat when you changed. I don't know how you did it?'

Bridget didn't want to think about eating live weasels. It disgusted her. Besides, her stomach was sore and she still felt queasy. And she was exhausted too. She really didn't fancy feeling like this every time she changed. 'Can I go back to my dormitory? I feel sick,' Bridget said to the Principal.

'Certainly Bridget. Excellent work today. In fact, once you've done your inner wolf class, you can have the rest of the day off. And no more shifts for you until Friday.'

Bridget exhaled as she said goodbye to everyone though Katy rushed after her to give her a last hug.

***

Birdget showered quickly, enjoying washing off the horrible bits of flesh and skin that were stuck to her body. Her mouth tasted of fur and she gagged. Bits of raw meat were stuck between her teeth so she let the shower water wash the inside of her mouth and it felt good. A bottle of mouth wash would get rid of the horrible taste. After she'd cleaned all her teeth, she lay in bed and thought about everything that had happened to her. She scowled when she remembered the pain of her body tearing itself apart. Looking down at her arms, she saw little bruises were already forming on her tingling skin.

'Bridget, please go to Miss Flanagan's office immediately,' a voice sounded over the intercom.

Bridget jerked on the bed and looked up in surprise at the intercom on the wall. She hadn't noticed it before and when she looked at her watch saw that it was ten minutes past two. She was already late for class. Hurrying down the stairs, she knocked tentatively on the door of the therapy room.

'Come in,' said Lou Flanagan in a warm voice.

Bridget walked in and slumped down on the chair. Lou looked over her glasses and smiled. 'I hear your shape shift went very well. Congratulations, Bridget. How do you feel?'

'Sick,' mumbled Bridget.

Lou looked away from Bridget and straightened the folder on her lap. 'It will take time, Bridget, but you will soon be very comfortable with it.' Lou sighed, 'Now, this class is all about loving your inner wolf.'

Bridget glowered and looked out the window. She knew she was being rude but couldn't help herself. A part of her wanted to stand up and scream out. 'But what if I don't want to love the wolf within?'

Lou started droning on. 'When we are wolves, we are majestic animals. We are at one with nature. We are instinctive and wild. Our power of reason subsides and we answer to the needs of our bodies.' Lou stared at Bridget impatiently and Bridget sat up a little. 'So tell me how you feel when you're a wolf.'

Bridget sniffed and considered her words carefully. 'I don't like it. Not one bit.'

'What don't you like about it?' asked Lou scribbling in her notepad.

'Well, everything really. I don't get the 'being at one with nature' part. I hate being out of control and animalistic. And I absolutely *hate* the smell of my body before and afterwards...'

An uneasy silence descended and Lou fiddled with her pen. 'Okay. Tell me about your childhood.'

Bridget's mouth tightened. 'If you're thinking that something happened during my childhood to make me this way, then well, you know, forget it!'

'I'm not thinking anything, Bridget. I'm simply trying to discover more about you. How did you get on with your father?'

Bridget's stomach tightened and she felt even more defensive. 'I got on really well with my Dad, you know. He was always very sympathetic whenever I had questions about being a werewolf.'

'I'm sure he was,' said Lou wryly. 'But did he encourage you?'

'He never said anything bad about it. He listened to my worries.'

'And what were those worries?'

Bridget desperately wanted to run out of the class. Someone she'd only met two days earlier was asking her to reveal her innermost thoughts. The clock chimed and Lou looked at it irritably. 'Our time is up. And just when we were getting to the interesting part. We'll continue this conversation at our next session.'

Getting up and hurrying out of the room, Bridget puffed out her cheeks and sighed. How was she expected to go through therapy *and* shape shifting? She had to get away from this school. But something else was nagging at her - all the teachers seemed to have a problem with her Dad. Why was that? The Principal had her Dad's file in her office. If Bridget wanted to find out more, she'd have to stay in the Institute.

But staying would be impossible. She remembered the fade drops in the lab. If she swallowed them, maybe instead of making her invisible, they might kill her. Wouldn't that be better than having to live like an animal for the rest of her life? She thought of her mother – could she really take that risk and leave her mother alone? But she was desperate to leave.

4

FADE DROPS

Very early next morning, Bridget rose from her bed and crept down the back stairs towards the lab. As she approached it, she looked from her left to her right, making sure that no one was about. What if the door was locked?

Reaching for the door handle, Bridget gently pulled it down and found to her relief that it opened. Walking quietly into the lab, she took a sniff of the wonderful smell of disinfectant. Bridget moved over to the side wall, where she'd seen Mr Boyle put the gloves. Crouching down and touching the skirting board gently, she ran her fingers along it. She felt a tiny groove under her finger and when she put pressure on it, the skirting board fell open.

Bridget exhaled, lifting her head up quickly to make sure that no one was watching her. Sticking her hand into the cavity behind the skirting, she felt the coarse material of the gloves. She pulled them out and glanced over at the door again. Her heart was racing now.

Walking over to the silver paned cabinet, Bridget put the gloves on and took the key out from its pocket. Her hands trembled as she opened the cabinet and peered inside. Carefully picking up a few bottles, Bridget saw the blue one marked 'fade drops' and her heart leapt in her chest. She noticed the odd garlic-shaped bottle and her eyes darted towards the door again. Why was this bottle so top-secret?

She picked it up and squinted at the label. The print was very small but she could make out the words 'Vampform.' What a strange name? What could it possibly be?

Then Bridget remembered that she'd only come into the lab to get the fade drops so she replaced the violet bottle and unscrewed the fade drops. The smell of honey and cinnamon wafted out.

Bridget's heart pounded in her chest and she looked at the label for instructions. There were none. Could she really drink this? It might kill her. And the Institute wasn't so bad, the others were fun and most of the lessons were hilarious. She even had a new best friend. The emotional roller coaster and the party were coming up. But shape shifting was brutal. Opening her mouth and placing the bottle against her quivering lips, Bridget swallowed a small mouthful. It tasted sweet and had a syrupy texture on her tongue. She waited and looked down at her hands. Was this going to kill her? Was she about to die?

Suddenly, Bridget looked down again and saw that her feet had disappeared. It was actually working! She looked at her hazy reflection on the glass of the lab cabinets and saw herself disappearing. Her heart hopped in her chest and she almost giggled out loud.

Bridget closed the cabinet door and replaced the gloves in the skirting board. In herself, she didn't feel any different at all though when she looked down, she couldn't see her body or her feet moving on the floor. Once out in the corridor, Bridget picked up a dirty bone from the floor. It hung in the air and she let out a laugh.

Thrilled, Bridget made her way to the front door but when she got to it, she saw that it was locked and there were no keys hanging near it. Maybe she could get out the windows? She ran over to the window and jabbed at the handle but it was locked too. There must be keys somewhere. Bridget stamped her invisible foot in frustration and then remembered that she'd seen Miss Joyce handing a clump of keys into the Principal's office the morning before. She raced down the corridor.

Once Bridget got into the Principal's office, she hurried over to the desk, frantically opening every drawer but there were no keys, only folders and pens. She looked at the walls for key racks. Seeing that the computer was on, Bridget watched as her invisible hand shifted the mouse on its pad. To her shock, the images that appeared on the screen were eight screens within one large one. Bridget gasped out loud. This was the security system for the whole school. The Principal hadn't told them that they were being filmed every day.

Bridget noticed the small box titled 'Principal's office' and saw that the time 6.03 am flashed underneath. Clicking on the image, a larger picture of the office came up. Swallowing hard, she zoomed in on the keyboard and jiggled the mouse and could see the movement of the mouse on the screen.

Bridget went back to the main menu and clicked on the image for the lab. Hitting the rewind button, she watched as the film reversed. When she saw herself enter the lab, her heart sank. If she didn't find the keys, she'd have to eliminate this evidence. She clicked onto the hall camera and saw herself rushing down to the lab. Deleting the minutes in the hall and the time in the lab was now an imperative. Luckily, she'd set up the cameras on *Howlo.*

Bridget cut and pasted the earlier time and overlaid it onto the moments when she appeared. Now, she clicked in and out of various security files to find the central locking system but soon realised that the doors and windows were operated the old fashioned way - with blasted keys.

Bridget returned to the main menu camera page when something very strange caught her eye. Katy and Eddie were sitting on a sofa with Lou Flanagan facing them. The Principal had obviously been reviewing this piece of film and saved it as a file. What could Katy and Eddie be doing together? Bridget clicked onto the image and let the film play. It was difficult to hear so she turned up the volume.

'Let's practice counting to ten again, Eddie,' Lou said encouragingly to a scowling Eddie.

Lou whispered. 'One, two, three. Now imagine, there's an Arsenal fan in front of you shouting that Chelsea are a rubbish team...keep counting...four, five...'

Eddie shifted uncomfortably on the sofa. Bridget squirmed when she saw a coy-looking Katy placing her hand on Eddie's arm. Eddie continued breathing heavily and fisting his hands. 'Get lost, you stupid blanker,' he growled at Lou, his fangs showing. Katy rubbed Eddie's left shoulder reassuringly and Bridget felt more confused. What is Katy doing at Eddie's anger management classes? And why hadn't she told Bridget?

Lou took a sharp breath and glared at Eddie. 'Calm down and let's start again. Maybe with a bit of visualisation this time.'

Lou continued, 'You're in a forest and the sun is shining. You've just had a lovely lunch of wild boar. You're feeling calm and relaxed. You lie down on the grass breathing in all the wonderful smells of flowers and forest. Slowly relax your breathing...slow it all down...four breaths in, one, two, three, four and exhale with six breaths, one, two, three, four, five, six...yes, lovely.'

Eddie now looked serene with his eyes closed and Katy tilted her head towards him and rubbed him.

Lou continued to murmur, 'you see the Arsenal supporter coming towards you but you don't react.' Eddie's breathing seemed still quite slow. 'He's walking over to you and he's extending his hand in friendship. You find yourself reaching your own hand towards him.'

Bridget watched as Eddie started to fidget. It was obvious he was trying to control his temper. 'You are looking into the Arsenal supporter's eyes and you're smiling at him.'

Suddenly Eddie began to pant and he lost control again. 'You are still calm. Breathe in for four, one, two, three, four. Breathe out for six, one, two, three, four, five, six...'

But it was too late, Eddie jumped up on his chair, his eyes flaring with rage. Lou sighed. Katy stood up and put her arm around Eddie.

Bridget watched in dismay, feeling utterly betrayed by Katy. She clicked out of the file in frustration and scrolled down on recent documents but stopped abruptly when she saw a file with her father's name. Her heart thumped.

Bridget clicked on the file and tugged at her invisible hair. It looked like something out of a spy movie with a 'top secret' crest in the centre. It was even encrypted. She'd need a password to open it. Bridget slammed her hand down on the mouse in anger. She looked down at a post-it on the desk and saw some scribbled writing, 'Patrick Quarry-French – member of the WEEsistance.' What is the WEEsistance?

Bridget's thoughts were interrupted by the sound of her stomach rumbling. And when she looked down, her feet were visible again. Her heart sank - she was starting to re-appear. What a fool she'd been spending so much time watching Katy and Eddie. She hadn't discovered anything new about her Dad and because she hadn't found the keys either, leaving the Institute was now impossible.

Bridget jumped up from the seat but then remembered that she needed to cover her tracks so she erased the last half hour in the Principal's office. From looking at the security files Bridget could tell that there were blind spots in the corridor, places the camera could not see. She'd just wait at one of those points until she was completely visible again and join the others as they came down for breakfast.

***

'Change of timetable this morning,' said Miss Joyce as they finished choir. 'Bridget, you and Katy have to watch wildlife DVDs for an hour. It's part of your therapy to help you develop a love of raw meat.'

Bridget looked across at Katy and scowled. She felt so hurt and conflicted now - like Katy had betrayed her. Eddie bullied her constantly and Bridget didn't understand why Katy was helping him with anything. And the most frustrating part was that Bridget couldn't say anything without admitting to seeing it all on the Principal's computer.

Katy strode over and placed an arm on Bridget's shoulder. Bridget shrugged it off. Katy looked surprised but seemed to recover quickly. 'I suppose you ain't exactly looking forward to this.'

'No, I'm not,' Bridget answered sharply.

Bridget walked ahead of Katy in the corridor and when they reached the study, she deliberately sat on a single armchair instead of the sofa. Katy seemed confused. 'I hate seeing some poor critter getting killed,' said Katy as she turned on the machine. 'You know that thug Eddie, keeps bringing these DVDs back to his room to watch them.'

Bridget's eyes flashed at the mention of Eddie's name and Katy fidgeted with her hands. 'I gotta tell you something Bridget but its top secret and you can't tell anyone else.'

Bridget sat up and stared at Katy. 'Go on,' she said coolly.

'Well, it's just that the Principal has asked me to become Eddie's sponsor at his anger management classes and she told me not to mention it to anyone.'

Bridget exhaled. Of course, Katy was being forced to spend time with Eddie. 'But couldn't you have said no?' asked Bridget, bewildered.

Katy sighed. 'I told her that I was mighty uncomfortable being around Eddie but she just insisted and I had no choice. She swore me to secrecy but you know, you are my best friend here and I really couldn't keep this from you any longer.'

Bridget looked at Katy intently, relieved to still have her as a friend. Then Bridget remembered the cameras and that the whole conversation was being filmed.

Katy started to giggle and sat on the arm of Bridget's chair. 'Eddie is such a joke at the anger management classes...'

Bridget tapped Katy on the arm. 'Come on Katy, let's watch these DVDs. We want that party at Halloween, don't we?'

***

Later in the study, when everyone was sending messages on *Howlo*, Bridget too was checking her messages. She'd put her two friends Alda and Sharon on high alert about a possible party at the Institute on Halloween night and they'd left numerous notes asking for more details. 'Have you heard from Helen recently?' Bridget asked Katy.

Katy shifted uncomfortably in her seat. 'Oh my, you just reminded me. I haven't heard from her in days. Maybe she's on vacation. I can check with my friend Luanne.'

'Bridget, someone called Sharon has just sent a request to be my friend. She says she knows you,' Andrew said smugly.

Bridget smirked. She'd sent Sharon Andrew's profile. 'Yes, you'll probably meet her at Halloween. She's great fun.'

Bridget looked over at Katy again. How happy she was that they hadn't fallen out. If it weren't for shape shifting, she'd actually want to be here. Earlier on, after making sure they were far from the cameras, Bridget had told Katy how desperately she wanted to run away. How terrified and traumatised she was by it all. Katy had pleaded with her to stay, reminding her about the stuff they had to look forward to. Bridget would only have a few more shape shifts to make before Halloween.

Katy seemed so upset at the thought of Bridget leaving, that Bridget had given in. And of course, she wanted to find out more about her Dad and the WEEsistance, whatever that was? She'd do her best to stay until Halloween, but after that, she was definitely getting out.

5

HALLOWEEN

Halloween morning dawned. Bridget's skin itched. She thought about everything that had happened during the week. Two more shape shifts had left her feeling more wretched than usual but because most of the students were making progress, Principal Goode was allowing the party to go ahead.

Bridget did have to grin when she thought about the Institute's therapies for helping students become 'balanced' werewolves. Andrew had been wuppy trained - the equivalent of puppy training. Most days, the teachers still had to stop him peeing in the classroom so they'd put some newspaper out and were moving it closer to the door. Soon the paper would be moving out into the corridor and then he could pee in the drain. The teachers had restricted his water intake when he was in human form so fewer trips to the toilet (or the paper) were required.

Dev's arms were covered in allergy patches while Mr Boyle tried to create a special vaccine to stop his fur allergy. To the extreme embarrassment of the girls, Roald continued to randomly lick their faces during class although he was down from twenty to ten licks a day.

Saori's mange had more or less cleared up but she still habitually scratched at her ears during class. With the help of Miss Joyce in Choir, Miguel's howl had gone from a whimper to a growl and Simonetta ate the live weasels once they were sprinkled with hamburger dressing. But Katy wasn't improving at all. She could shape shift no problem but she still didn't eat the raw meat. Bridget wondered why she hadn't lost any weight given how little she ate. And Eddie, well Bridget didn't like thinking about him. He was his usual self, a really unpalatable combination of taunting aggressiveness.

Bridget pictured what she had to do tonight. The full moon would force her to shape shift automatically and that made her think about running away again. She'd been watching the Principal for days now. She brought the door keys to her room every night. Bridget would just have to take a few fade drops and steal the keys from her room tomorrow morning. But something still bothered her. What was this WEEsistance that her Dad had been a member of? If she stayed at the Institute longer, she could find that out. And also she felt lonely when she thought of leaving Katy. She loved Katy and (except for Eddie), she really did like the rest of her class so much.

Bridget ran into the bathroom and looked at herself in the mirror. Nothing was obviously different until she poked at her nose and saw the familiar sprigs of hair growing under her nostrils. She clicked her tongue in annoyance and patted her night gown. Running her fingers under her armpits, beads of sweat trickled down. She looked over at Katy, Simonetta and Saori, as they continued to sleep on their straw. For Bridget, this was the worst part about being a werewolf, the lack of control over her body. In a few hours time, she'd be a werewolf again.

Biting her lip, Bridget rushed into the shower to wash off some of the smell from her body. She wouldn't be shape shifting until they got to Mallow Castle. It was time to forget about it and think instead about the fun of the emotional rollercoaster. Classes were finishing at 4.00pm to allow the students to freshen up before they left for Mallow town. Andrew had compiled a brilliant playlist for the party with at least five hours of music.

At 4 o'clock, the howl sounded and the class ran gleefully up the stairs to the showers. All day, Bridget felt the inevitable stretch of her skin, her body getting ready to shape shift. She took a sniff of her body and smelled again the strong body odour that always preceded the metamorphosis.

'Bridget, have you got my *She* perfume, in there?' enquired Saori, through the locked toilet door.

'Yeah, just giving myself a little squirt and I'll be with you in a minute.'

Bridget came out of the toilet and the other whooped at her in admiration. She'd sprayed the hair over her left ear a luminous pink and a ring with a large oval orange stone flashed on her finger. Saori bit her lip and scratched behind her ear.

'Wow, Bri-geet, you look *bella*,' said Simonetta. 'Can you tie this for me please?'

Bridget bristled with pride as she strode over to Simonetta to fasten her leopard print necklace. Katy came out of the shower and put on a tiny giraffe-skin skirt drawing a couple of admiring gasps from the girls. A bowing Saori wore a checked bandana, orange hot pants and painted-on orange nails for the night.

Bridget nodded at the girls. 'Are we ready?' Everyone rushed towards the door giggling. They opened the dormitory door to find the boys waiting for them – along with an overpowering smell of aftershave.

Bridget giggled, 'You scrub up well, lads. Are we ready to party?'

Andrew looked charming in a dark-blue beanie with the Herr Wolf logo on the front. Roald was wearing a tiger print watch with a matching armband, his tongue flicking around his mouth. Eddie had dyed his mullet orange and looked surprisingly handsome. Katy rushed over to him and gave him a hug. As all their voices were beginning to change, they let out a massive howl, 'Awhooooooooo!' and charged towards the bus.

Lou Flanagan sat in the driver's seat and grinned as they approached. 'You all look gorgeous and handsome. Wonderful, just wonderful. The food is stunning this year, students. You will not be disappointed.'

Bridget felt a knot in her stomach. She needed to stop thinking about the coming change and concentrate instead on all the fun they'd be having tonight. She watched the others climb onto the bus jostling and pushing good heartedly and then the bus set off.

It was the first time that Bridget had been outside the grounds of the Institute since she arrived and she peered out the bus window inquisitively. She saw a mother and her two children, dressed as Halloween witches, running up the road shrieking with laugher. On the outskirts of Mallow town, everyone cheered when they saw the red and yellow sign for the Circus.

'Quickly Miss Flanagan, we need to go on the emotional rollercoaster before we shape shift,' said Bridget eagerly.

'Don't worry. You won't change until we get to Mallow castle. The circus doesn't open for another two hours. We paid Mr Cody a little bit extra for exclusive use of his rollercoaster.'

Everyone screamed with excitement. Lou parked the car and they skipped towards the entrance. A squat man wearing a theatrical red suit stood at the front and over his head the sign read, 'Emotional Rollercoaster.'

'Have you signed all the consent forms?' he asked Lou sternly.

'Yes, we have,' said Lou with authority.

'OK then, come on in,' he smiled, his nose twitched as the students passed him.

There was a scramble among them to get to the front of the queue until Lou announced, 'This was Bridget's idea and I think she should be in the first carriage.'

Bridget took her ticket first from Mr Cody and when he wrinkled his nose, Bridget knew it was because of her body odour. Everyone followed Bridget inside a tiny dark cave that within seconds revealed a small train with individual carriages for four people. In the distance, they saw an enormous wheel.

Bridget sat into a plump-cushioned red seat in the first carriage, giddy with excitement. Katy rushed to sit behind her. Eddie and Andrew sat opposite them while Roald, Saori, Miguel and Dev took the second carriage.

Simonetta stood forlornly on the platform. 'Squeeze in with Roald,' said Bridget enthusiastically.

Mr Cody positioned himself beside them on the track, blinking and waving his left hand as if he was doing a waltz. He spoke in a rolling theatrical voice. 'The Emotional Roller Coaster is the world's greatest ride. At the back of each of your seats, is a headset. When you put your headsets on, the film you see and the music you hear will evoke many different emotions, enhancing your experience on the emotional rollercoaster.'

Suddenly he dropped the flourishing vowels and became stern. 'Do not attempt to open your harness during the ride as this would be extremely dangerous. Enjoy the ride!' He shuffled away from the train with Lou following.

Bridget squealed and grabbed her headset, placing the ear plugs over her ears and adjusting the screen in front of her eyes. Then she gripped the hand rail as the train jerked to a start. The train picked up speed and vaulted down the track. Whoops of laughter rose as it accelerated. On Bridget's screen, an image of a horse trotted down the road to jaunty, light-hearted music. Katy squeezed Bridget's hand and giggled. Bridget looked across at Eddie, his face ecstatic. For the first time since he'd arrived at the Institute, Eddie actually looked happy.

Suddenly, the train hit a bend and the image changed to an army running over a hill to the sound of thundering gun fire and opera. Bridget's body pumped with adrenalin and her heart pounded in her chest. She clenched her jaw, feeling as if she wanted to kill someone. Eddie banged his fists against the handrail and screamed profanities at the top of his voice. Suddenly, Bridget felt a slap sting her face and she recoiled. Katy had just hit her. Bridget heard Dev sneezing violently behind her and she felt something wet hit the back of her hair.

They flew around another corner, the skin on their faces pressed back by the force of the wind. The music changed to a slow and sad melody, and the image turned to a child at a funeral saying goodbye to her dead father. Bridget thought of her own father's funeral and couldn't hold in her wailing cries. Tears streamed down the faces of Katy, Eddie and Andrew and their bodies shook with grief. Eddie's body was slouched and he looked as if he would never recover from his desolation.

The train rattled on the track. Suddenly they started to climb upwards, an image of bulls running down a street behind them. The noise was deafening. Bridget bit her lips and clutched her arms to her chest in fear.

Once they got to the top of the roller coaster, the image changed to a child on Christmas Day getting all the presents she'd ever wanted. Bridget felt like her heart would burst with happiness. Everyone else was laughing hysterically and cheering. Around the bend they went again, to an image of a child eating a piping hot dinner while another child in the street outside had its face pressed to the window, watching enviously. Katy dug her nails into Bridget's arm and Bridget yelled in pain. What was wrong with Katy, why was she taking out her anger on Bridget?

Bridget felt a splash of water hit her face. She looked across and saw that Andrew's trousers were sopping wet and she flinched, knowing full well what she was covered with. Although the train moved into all the different states and had a mood swing on every corner, Eddie continued to hold his sides and laugh hysterically. Eventually, with a lobster red face, he panted at Bridget, 'I can't stop, I'm stuck on happy. Help me!'

At that moment, the train shuddered to a halt and the students sat in their carriages looking utterly exhausted. Eddie continued to laugh uncontrollably, rolling around on the carriage seat. Everyone watched him with surprise. Bridget stood up and stumbled out. She could see Roald's red face as he struggled to lift himself off the carriage. All his clothes were wet. Even though, he looked tired, he grinned. 'I'm covered in Dev's snot and Andrew's urine,' he guffawed.

Bridget touched the back of her hair and felt something sticky - she shuddered. She looked over at Eddie who was still in hysterics. 'He certainly had a great time, didn't he?' she said.

Katy appeared annoyed. 'I'm sure he'll snap out of it soon,' she said gruffly.

Mr Cody arrived along the track, hearing Katy. 'Yes, don't worry. He'll be back to normal in a moment or two. Did you enjoy yourselves?'

'Yes,' everyone chorused wholeheartedly.

Roald and Andrew groaned. 'What a pity we can't keep Eddie like this forever. He's much better fun.'

Almost at once, Eddie stopped laughing and sniffed. Then he narrowed his eyes and his mouth tightened. 'What are you freaks looking at? When we going to the castle?'

'We're leaving immediately,' said Lou.

Bridget grabbed Katy's arm but Katy pushed her away. Bridget had never seen Katy like this before. If Eddie couldn't get past laughter, it seemed Katy was stuck on fury.

***

Arriving into Mallow town, they drove past a towering stone statue on Thomas Davis Street. 'That's the J.J. Fitzgerald monument,' said Lou.

They passed a beautiful clock tower in the centre of the town. Then they took a left to Spa Square and on to Bridewell Lane before arriving at the entrance of Mallow Castle. On the large brass gates, the deer-head emblem hung solemnly. With a click of Lou's zapper, the gates creaked open. She drove in, slowly, stopping beside a forest and turning off the engine. Everyone disembarked speedily.

Lou gestured to them, 'Perhaps if you want to divide into two groups, left and right? There are more than three hundred deer here so no need to rush. I've also taken the liberty of ordering some barking attendants for you. There is a family living in the castle, you know. And your sense of smell will not be optimal because of the odour from the cheese in the river, so the hounds will make sure you aren't disturbed.' Lou whistled sharply and the sound of dogs running towards them on the gravel path could be heard.

'Meet Ben, Len and Glen.' Everyone barked and the hounds gave a little whimper. They looked a little intimidated to be standing so close to seven almost-wolves.

'Hello, cousins,' squealed Bridget, sending them all an air kiss. The hounds licked Bridget's boots, relieving the tension and making her giggle.

'Ben, can you position yourself near the gate please? Len, if you could please follow the males to the left and Glen, can you stand guard over to the right near the she-wolves, please?' said Lou. All the hounds barked in unison and sauntered alongside the wolf packs.

'Just one last thing, run into the farthest part of the forest and try to shape shift as quietly as possible,' Lou said as she walked back to the bus.

Bridget and the other females ran off the path. Saori and Simonetta raced ahead but Katy stayed close to Bridget. They ran for about five minutes and then stopped beside a pond. Bridget looked across at Katy. 'I don't really want to do this but I can't stop it now. Are you ready?'

Katy scowled and she and Bridget took their shoes off. The moon came out from behind the clouds and Bridget dropped on all fours onto the grass. She started to howl and as she looked over at Katy, she saw that Katy's brown eyes had changed to a lime green colour. Both of them were groaning loudly as the skin on their backs began to crack and blood oozed out. Bridget heard her clothes tear off her body and she looked down at her expanding rib cage and moaned. Her spine began to arch and lengthen and the muscles in her legs and arms started to throb and pulse. Her heart pounded in her ears and her body shook uncontrollably.

A long snout shot out of Bridget's face and her nostrils flared over gleaming fangs. She gnashed as her neck extended and her shoulders broadened. Flexing her hands, they changed into long paws with sharp nails on the end of each claw. Hair grew quickly all over her face, her arms, her legs and her back. The distorted reflection in the water of the lake showed no sign of a human. Bridget was an animal now.

Bridget's heart raced, the familiar hunger for flesh began. Snarling and tossing her head from side to side, the savage animal she'd just become urgently need to hunt.

***

The boys sprang from the gravel path into the trees following the scent of the deer. Roald went first, springing ahead. His large incisors and front paws grabbed the flesh of a large male and he bit deeply into the deer's neck with his powerful jaw muscles. The animal struggled at first, terrified, urinating all over Roald's hind legs, but within seconds the deer's life had ended. Andrew, Dev and Eddie ran up behind Roald to share the meal. Soon the forest was full of muted sounds of munching and crunching.

***

Bridget ran ahead but Katy hung back. Bridget twisted her head around and sniffed sharply at Katy. Then she dipped her head and looked ahead of her again. Katy came closer to Bridget's body and Bridget jerked out of the way to avoid contact. It felt like Katy was challenging her. Bridget looked at Katy and snarled. Katy showed her fangs. Bridget couldn't believe it. Was Katy going to attack? She'd been acting very strangely on the bus. Something was definitely wrong with her. Bridget growled at Katy, asserting herself but Katy simply began to circle her. She *was* getting ready to attack. Bridget's breathing grew faster, she snarled again but Katy didn't back down.

Suddenly, Katy vaulted towards Bridget, talons extended. Katy's claws tore through the fur on Bridget's back and slashed her flesh. Bridget felt the pain as Katy's nails dug into her body and blood gushed out of the wound. Bridget staggered against the bark of a tree and pushed Katy off her, feeling completely terrorised. Suddenly, Bridget heard someone shouting, 'Stop!'

Katy rolled over on the grass as Bridget looked up to see the impossible - VAMPIRES. She'd only ever seen pictures of them in books. The moonlight reflected off their pale skin, their eyes were hypnotic and their teeth pointy. A gurgle escaped from Bridget's throat. There were three of them perched on a branch of a tree circling Bridget and Katy. Bridget felt her heart go into overdrive. She and Katy were outnumbered. The vampires could swoop down any second and kill them. Katy turned her snarling jaws upward and stopped dead when she saw them.

The vampire who'd just asked them to stop fighting was a girl who whizzed from branch to branch. Beside her, a dark skinned vampire with lime green nails grinned down at Bridget and Katy. The third vampire, wobbled on his branch, looking like he might fall off but he said nothing. Bridget sniffed deeply, they smelled really clean and their teeth were dazzling.

Katy howled loudly to alert the other werewolves. The nervous-looking vampire girl looked down at Bridget and spoke falteringly. 'Hi. I'm Molly. It looked like you needed a bit of help there.'

Bridget couldn't believe it – a helpful vampire. But wait maybe it was just a trap. Perhaps this clever vampire was trying to lure Bridget into a false sense of security so that she could fly down and bite her. They loved blood and Bridget was covered in it. Bridget put her paw on her throat defensively. She could hear the other werewolves running towards them and she suddenly felt safer.

6

Bridget meets the Vampires

Lou ran towards Bridget, stopping directly in front of her. Eddie, Roald, Andrew, Miguel, Dev, Simonetta and Saori all arrived together. Now it was the vampires who looked intimidated. Len, Ben and Glen scurried up to the group and barked uncontrollably.

Lou looked at Bridget's gushing wound and with trembling hands said. 'Did they attack you?'

'Yes,' panted Katy. 'They attacked Bridget.'

Bridget looked at Katy incredulously as Eddie and Roald howled and got ready to move into the pounce position.

'We didn't attack her,' said the vampire, who'd introduced herself as Molly, her eyes flaring with indignity. A chorus of ferocious growls rose up from the werewolves.

'It was Katy,' blurted Bridget. 'Katy attached me.'

Everyone looked at Katy in confusion and Lou's eyes widened. 'Katy, what's going on? Did you attack Bridget?'

'I swear I didn't, it was them,' Katy said raising her paw at the vampires.

'No, we didn't,' shouted a vampire behind Molly with an American accent. 'You did it.'

Suddenly, the wobbly vampire slumped forward, hit a large branch and fell to the ground with a loud thud. The electric tension in the air snapped as he began to snore loudly. Bridget looked from Molly to the werewolves and screwed up her face. No one knew what to do.

Molly's soft Irish voice pleaded from the tree. 'We only tried to help Bridget, we promise. Please don't touch Vlad. He's narcoleptic. '

Roald and Andrew growled in condescension and Bridget watched as Molly's face turned sad. Bridget couldn't explain why but she felt sorry for Molly. Despite herself, Bridget started to step backwards. Eddie growled at Bridget to stay put.

Lou wagged her finger at her students. 'No one move! Andrew and Roald, help Bridget back to the bus. I have a first aid kit there.'

The werewolves circled Bridget, keeping their eyes on the vampires. Lou looked at the vampires. 'You will have to answer to Professor Prosperus for this breach. You'd better wake your friend up quickly. I know that your punishment will be very harsh if any of the locals see you.' She turned to her wolves, 'Back to the bus immediately.'

Bridget wanted to argue with Lou about Katy but the pain in her side was getting worse. She threw her paws over Andrew and Roald and hobbled along between them. When she took her paw away from the wound, it bled so strongly she had to lean it against Andrew. The pain stung but she knew she would heal quickly once Lou put a bandage on it. She looked across at Katy. What was wrong with her? She was lying about the vampires attacking. Bridget looked back quickly to see the dark vampire with luminous nails whistling while Molly whizzed from branch to branch above their crumpled snoring lump of a friend.

Hysterical chatter erupted as the others trailed behind Bridget. Lou shouted back angrily. 'Not another word.' And everyone shut up immediately.

When they had got back to the bus, there was an explosion of conversation.

'Lay Bridget down here,' ordered Lou.

Bridget's body was tugged about as they laid her flat on the floor of the bus. Lou grabbed the red first aid kit behind the passenger seat. She pulled out some white gauze, cotton cool and a bottle of disinfectant. 'Does it hurt, Bridget?'

'Not so much now.'

'You're probably already starting to heal.'

Lou dabbed at the wound with the disinfectant and Bridget tensed up. 'Oooh, that stings!' she said squeezing her eyes shut.

The others stopped talking and looked on concerned. Roald gave Bridget a lick but she didn't mind at all.

'I'm going to put some instant stitches on the wound. They will repair everything quickly. Hold still a while longer.'

Bridget stopped wriggling as Andrew rubbed her forehead. Katy was nowhere near.

'OK, that's done,' said Lou after a few minutes. 'I put a little of Mr Boyle's accelerated grazing tincture on it too. You'll need to take it easy tonight but by tomorrow you'll be right as rain.'

'Thanks Lou,' said Bridget pulling herself up. The pain wasn't gone, but it wasn't more than she could handle.

'Let's go back to the Institute,' said Lou as she slammed the bus door closed. 'We'll get to the bottom of this when we get home.'

As they set off, Bridget stared at Katy in bewilderment, but Katy didn't meet her eye, spending the whole time looking out the window in silence.

Roald and Andrew didn't seem bothered by the tension on the bus and chatted noisily. 'Did you see that? A vampire who falls asleep all the time – how pathetic is he?' Roald roared with laughter.

In spite of her worries about Katy, Bridget couldn't help feel curious about Molly the vampire who shockingly, had tried to protect her. It was very unvampire-like behaviour. Weren't they supposed to hate werewolves?

Lou drove through the gates, scanning the trees. 'Those vampires have probably gone. I simply can't understand how they managed to cross the river. This is a very serious breach. We'll have to call an emergency meeting with the Principal.'

Bridget frowned. 'Does that mean the party is off?' The others leaned forward and waited.

Lou turned the steering wheel to the right. 'Let's get back to the Institute first and we'll see. It's far too dangerous to stay around Mallow now.'

Lou dialled the Principal's mobile number. 'Miriam, I mean...Principal. There's been a vampire breach at the castle. Bridget was attacked and injured. Can you meet us in the infirmary?'

The Principal's voice sounded tense over the loud speaker, 'Oh, my goodness. No problem Miss Flanagan. Is Bridget okay?'

Lou frowned. 'She's fine. We will see you in five.'

***

When they arrived at the Institute and got out of the bus, Roald and Andrew linked Bridget in their arms. Principal Goode and Mr Boyle waited at the infirmary, looking very concerned. The Principal rushed forward and Mr Boyle lead Bridget to one of the beds to examine her wound.

'Good job, Lou. I couldn't have done better myself. I see my improved grazing salve is working miracles already. Well done.'

The Principal waited and watched. All the students chatted as Bridget got up from the bed.

The Principal folded her arms over her chest defensively. 'Now that we've established that Bridget is well, I want a full report of what happened. Lou?'

'There seems to be a little confusion,' said Lou looking from Bridget to Katy.

'Bridget is saying that Katy attacked her and Katy maintains that it was the vampires who did it.'

'It was Katy,' said Bridget assertively.

The Principal looked at Katy. 'Did you attack Bridget?'

'No,' said Katy. 'It was those vicious vampires.'

Bridget couldn't understand why Katy was lying. 'You know you did it Katy. Why keep denying it?' She looked around the room and saw that everyone wanted to believe Katy, wanted to believe that the vampires attacked.

'Of course, it was the vampires. You're just confused Bridget,' the Principal said impatiently.

Bridget began to feel upset thinking about the attack again. And then she remembered something. 'Check under Katy's nails.'

Katy looked horrified and the Principal clicked her tongue. 'Really Bridget, there is no point in continuing this charade. Katy, show me your paws.'

Katy seemed reluctant to give the Principal her paw but when she did the Principal's mouth dropped wide open. Everyone leaned in and could see bits of fur, flesh and blood attached to Katy's nails. 'How did that get there?' asked the Principal.

'Oh my. I sure don't remember,' Katy said looking embarrassed.

Bridget felt a mixture of relief and confusion.

'It's the emotional roller coaster. She must have got stuck on angry,' Eddie butted in.

Everyone looked at Lou. 'Well, actually that would be one explanation. Eddie was stuck on happy for a while afterwards.' She looked at Katy. 'Do you think that's it, Katy?'

Katy nodded. 'It must be. I'm all confused. Bridget is my best friend. I could never hurt her.' Katy rushed over to Bridget to give her a hug. Bridget was slow to hug her back. It did explain Katy's savage behaviour. Bridget had felt a little weird herself after the ride ended.

The Principal looked irritated. 'Now we've got that sorted. How did the vampires cross the river?'

'It appears they've managed to counteract the *Godwin's* garlic formula,' Lou replied.

Mr Boyle snarled. 'But how? Have they developed a recipe themselves?'

The Principal eyed her students. 'Can you give me a description of the perpetrators? Bridget?'

Bridget wanted to smile but didn't. 'Oh yes, Principal. There was a very dark vampire wearing lime-green nail varnish and a gold chain. A vampire called Vlad who actually fell asleep and dropped out of the tree while we were standing there... and an Irish female vampire called Molly.'

The Principal scribbled in her notebook. 'And what did she say?'

'Molly stopped Katy attacking me.'

'I'm sure the vampire didn't,' said the Principal irritably.

'Why won't you believe anything I've said?' said Bridget looking around at everyone. 'Molly did stop it.'

None of them appeared prepared to believe that three vampires had saved Bridget from Katy. They needed to believe that vampires were the enemy.

The Principal huffed in annoyance and patted her chest. 'Whatever you say, Bridget. We can't do anything now, but I will phone the Head of the United Supernatural Nations, Mr Zen Chow. We need to convene a meeting.' The Principal straightened herself up. 'Lou, report this problem to the circus master. And now, I suggest that we forget about this incident and enjoy the party. Bridget, you'll need to forego dancing tonight and mind your injury.'

A screech of brakes interrupted the conversation and everyone looked out the window. 'I see Miss Joyce has just arrived with our visitors.'

As the students headed for the door, the Principal added. 'And by the way, under no circumstances are you allowed to discuss what occurred tonight. This is private Institute business.'

7

THE PARTY

Bridget ran ahead of the others to greet the new arrivals. There was a huge amount of scrambling at the front entrance. Alda, Sharon and Rose were dressed up to the nines and each of them wore a brightly coloured hair-band between their furry ears. Katy stayed close to Bridget as she introduced her friends.

'What happened to your back?' Alda asked, pointing at Bridget's bandage.

Bridget looked uncertainly at Katy. 'Oh, I just got spiked by a deer's antlers while we were in the park.'

'Does it hurt?' asked Rose patting Bridget's fur.

'Not really. I can't do much dancing tonight though because I might strain my stitches.' Alda and Rose nudged Bridget with their heads in an attempt to cheer her up.

Katy looked apologetically at Bridget. 'I'm so sorry Bridget. I didn't mean to hurt you,' she whispered.

Bridget took in Katy's sorrowful face and realised that Katy was truly sorry. 'Let's forget about it, okay.'

Andrew, Roald, Miquel and Dev seemed delighted to be meeting some outsiders. Roald's tongue hung out and Alda burst out laughing. Andrew hopped from one foot to the other and rushed in to start the music. Everyone cheered when they came into the hall. It was a riot of black and orange with pumpkin lanterns all along the walls. Roald and Simonetta had been put in charge of decorating and Simonetta had ordered a black disco ball with shards of orange mirrors which was now suspended from the central light. It reflected off the walls, throwing shapes of moons and pumpkins on to the bodies of the wolves.

Bridget squealed with pleasure as Andrew played 'Flame' by Bell X1 to start the music. Even though she'd been warned not to dance, she moved beside Sharon and Alda and began to wave her right paw back and forth. Katy didn't know the song but all the local wolves sang the chorus.

*'I want to be near you and blink in your light
and toast marshmallows on a cold dark night,
By your Flame...'*

Andrew puffed out his chest with the enthusiastic reaction. He'd only played two tracks and everyone was on the floor, even Eddie.

Bridget shouted encouragement. 'Come on wolves, hoooowwwwl.'

The students howled so loudly that the disco ball swung overhead, threatening to crash to the ground. Miguel managed a strong howl for the first time in ages and he beamed at his classmates. Eddie grinned and moved over beside Katy, inviting her to join him. She danced over to him, shimmying next to his hind leg.

'Bridget,' shouted Alda. 'I need to go to the loo, you coming?' Bridget nodded.

Katy followed quickly behind them. In the toilet, Bridget squealed with excitement, her tail hitting the door. 'Alda, this is my new friend, Katy. She's from Nashville.'

Bridget looked in the mirror and smoothed the fur on her pink ear, 'What's with you and Eddie? You're getting a bit close to him, aren't you?'

Katy rolled her eyes in mock horror. 'Principal's orders. Please help me get away from that weirdo!'

Bridget chuckled. 'I'm having so much fun even Eddie doesn't bother me tonight. The dancing doesn't really hurt. I might even help you out and dance with *him*.'

'Bridget honey, you're such a pal,' said Katy running a comb along her fur.

'Maybe I'll dance with him too,' added Alda hopefully.

Bridget and Katy looked at each other and burst out laughing. 'Eddie is an acquired taste,' said Bridget.

'Especially if your taste runs to thug...' giggled Katy.

'What about the guy with the tongue, Roald?' interrupted Alda.

Bridget squirted some perfume on her chest fur, 'Off limits I'm afraid. He's Simonetta's. She told me yesterday that she likes him. What about Dev?' Bridget fixed her ear one more time.

'Which one is Dev?' asked Sharon.

'He's the gorgeous Indian guy,' said Bridget.

'Oh him! All that sneezing, I'm not sure I could cope. I think I'll give him a miss,' said Sharon giggling.

'He's actually really sweet,' Bridget sighed. 'Come on, let's hit the floor again.'

When they returned to the hall, the snacks were being served. Andrew lowered the music so that everyone could hear each other speak. An enormous aluminium bowl was piled high with juicy bones. Bridget stood up to make a speech. 'I think you'll all agree that these were just what we needed to clean our teeth with. Thanks Dev.' Everyone clapped and whistled and Dev wiped his snotty face coyly.

After everyone had finished chewing on their bones Andrew shouted, 'Now back to the music.' He turned the volume up again and played 'Born to be Wild' by Stefanwolf, the anthem of all wolves. Everyone, including Bridget growled with pleasure and gyrated on the floor. Roald and Dev moved into the centre of the dance floor and shook their tails back and forth. Bridget danced very tamely next to Katy, Alda, Sharon and Rose. She sure didn't want to burst her stitches.

'Is it sore?' asked Rose pointing at Bridget's injury.

'It's not bad at all,' Bridget lied. Bridget thought about sitting down but if this was her last rehab party, she certainly wasn't going to miss a second of it.

Andrew made a gleeful announcement. 'Okay. Let's do some scratch dancing.'

Everyone howled with joy because this was a classic werewolf dance. Bridget, Alda, Rose, Sharon and Katy squealed as they rushed into the centre of the dance floor, making up one row. Opposite them stood Roald, Dev, Eddie, Miquel and Andrew. In time with the music, they took three steps in and three steps back. At the chorus, the male and female dancers extended their paws and scratched their partner's fur. This led to the most hysterical scenes of fur rubbing amid roars of laughter. Roald scratched Bridget. She squirmed and giggled so much that she fell onto the floor in uncontrollable laughter shouting, 'stop, stop!'

'Eliminated!' shouted Saori, who was clearly dying to be scratched because she hurried in to take Bridget's place.

Everyone continued the dance while Bridget pulled herself up from the floor. In fits of laughter, she noticed a little blood blotted her bandage. She must have broken one of her stitches during the scratch dancing but she didn't care - it'd been worth it.

She looked out the window and noticed some little green lights twinkling outside. Simonetta hadn't mentioned putting fairy lights on the trees. She almost jumped out of her skin when she saw a set of dazzling teeth and a vampire's face grinning back at her. Molly had come to the school!

Bridget looked at the others. What could she do? She didn't really want to interrupt the scratch dancing because she knew what everyone's reaction would be to the vampires. She wanted to talk to the vampires again, and despite the danger, she tiptoed outside, her heart in her mouth.

**

'What do you want?' Bridget asked, her voice trembling as she hugged the door, just in case.

'We don't want any trouble. We're just checking to see that you're okay,' said Molly appealingly, flitting from one branch to the other.

Bridget stared up at Molly. She could see her more clearly now. She had short black hair and the usual deathly vampire palour. Her lips were bright red and her long nails (though two on each hand were very short) resembled pieces of cut glass flashing when she moved. But Molly's eyes were the most magnificent thing about her - a piercing, luminous blue. Molly's concern tugged at Bridget's heart a little.

'I'm fine, thanks so much for helping me earlier,' said Bridget.

'Is she really your friend?' said Molly pointing at Katy through the window.

'Oh, she didn't mean to do it...she just had a problem with, well, anyway.'

Molly looked back at Bridget again and fidgeted with her hands. 'The dancing looks like so much fun.' The other two vampires nodded but said nothing.

Suddenly, Bridget heard the males inside howling in alarm. Then she heard the assembly doors banging as everyone raced out. She turned to look back and saw Roald and Eddie's snarling jaws approaching her. Bridget felt very frightened but not for her own safety, for Molly's.

Eddie shoved Bridget out of the way when he leapt through the entrance doors. 'I'm going to rip your heads off, you stinking vampires!.'

Katy grabbed Bridget and pushed her behind Eddie. Bridget squirmed away from Katy just as Eddie went to pounce on the bark of the trees. Molly and the other vampires flew higher up on the branches and glared down. Roald, Andrew, Dev and Miquel snarled and tossed their heads defiantly.

'I am Vlad, top footballer from junior Russian league.' Vlad said, clearly trying to impress the werewolves. Eddie's ears pricked up at the mention of football.

Bridget stared at Vlad as he spoke. He was even more striking than Molly with beautiful full lips and high cheekbones. Bridget smiled nervously at him. Although she'd enjoyed all the wildness of the dancing, she wished the vampires could see her in human form.

'I'm Willy, a rapper from New York and your music is off the chart,' said the brown-eyed vampire, waving his green nails about.

Andrew lifted his hind leg and peed against the tree but Eddie continued to growl with fury. Bridget knew the situation could very quickly get out of hand. 'Thanks for coming by to see if I'm alright but it would be best if you left now.'

The werewolves jeered and Eddie made to climb up the tree. Bridget screamed, 'Just go now!' She couldn't quite believe that she'd just tried to protect the vampires but the thought of Eddie ripping Molly apart terrified her.

Molly looked down tenderly at Bridget and whispered. 'Thanks, Bridget.'

With a whish of the branches, Molly, Vlad and Willy flew away.

'What the...?' asked a bewildered Sharon.

'We met them earlier in Mallow Castle,' explained Bridget. 'They don't mean any harm.'

'What's wrong with you Bridget,' Eddie shouted, shoving her aggressively with his body. 'You forget that vampires are our oldest enemies?'

Bridget felt anxious and looked over at Katy. 'They only came to make sure I was okay.'

'You don't think we believe that, do you? They came here to kill you,' Eddie snarled.

Bridget rubbed the tip of her moist nose and Alda threw her paw around her shoulder.

Katy nudged Eddie with her head and drawled. 'Show's over folks, why don't we all go back inside.'

Andrew started up the music again but the crowd could do nothing but gossip and speculate about the vampires. Roald and Dev went to find the Principal, who came into the hall, looking highly agitated.

'The party's over, students. We cannot risk any deaths here tonight. Those vampires might come back in larger numbers so we are taking no chances. We hope you've all had a great night.'

Bridget said goodbye to the visitors and walked towards the dormitory. Everyone chatted incessantly about the vampires and the party but Bridget didn't feel like talking. Her mind was full of questions. She'd decided she wanted to leave the Institute but after meeting the vampires, she realised that a part of her now wanted to stay. But shape shifting made her life hell. Vampires or not - she had to go.

8

Arrival of Mr Chow

At 6 am, Bridget woke with a start. She lay naked on the hay, her human form restored. Shivering, she realised how cold the air was without fur. Not wanting to disturb the others, she dressed quietly and shot a longing look at Katy's bed.

As it was still dark outside, finding her way down the steps was difficult and Bridget stumbled a couple of times on her way to the lab. Once inside, she found the gloves and opened the cabinet quickly. There was no hesitation this time and she greedily gulped down the fade drops, swallowing a lot more than before.

Running down the corridor, Bridget climbed up the stairs to the Principal's bedroom to find the door slightly open. Her heart raced. Pushing back the door slowly, she saw a hay and normal bed. Luckily, Principal Goode wasn't in. Bridget sighed and glanced over at the bedside cabinet. Maybe the Principal has left the keys here?

Bridget opened the drawer and her heart almost stopped. Staring up at her was a file titled, 'Patrick Quarry-French, head of the Wee-sistance.' She picked it up and with trembling hands, opened it. Some of the pages had been torn out, but 'Date of Disappearance: 1 September 2010,' was scribbled on the back. Bridget sat immobile pondering what it all meant for her father had died on the 1st of September, not disappeared.

The clock on the bedside cabinet struck 6.30 am and Bridget suddenly remembered why she was in the Principal's bedroom - to run away from rehab. The keys must be down in the Principal's office.

When Bridget got there, the door was open. Craning her neck and looking inside, she was relieved to find it empty. As she was tearing the room apart searching for the keys, she suddenly heard the sound of approaching voices. Principal Goode was coming back to her office and Bridget had no way out. She ran behind the door, her back to the wall and watched as the most extraordinary person she'd ever seen came in the room with the Principal.

'Sit, sit, Mr Chow,' said Principal Goode warmly.

A figure moving like an octopus, wafted in to the room. He wore a long white kaftan over his large blob-like form. Bridget shuddered as her eyes caught sight of four massive tentacles poking out for legs. Not only that, at the end of each arm, he had tentacle fingers. On his head, a large cavity replaced his mouth with a smaller one for his nose. But the most striking thing about him was his eye. It was purple and had grown out of an antennae-like stalk at the top of his head. This must be Mr Chow, the head of the United Supernatural Nations. He was in charge of everything supernatural - (werewolves, vampires, aliens, anything non-human). There was a rumour going around that he was half-alien and half-Chinese but his alien side had definitely taken over.

'I have already phoned the Professor and he will be here shortly,' said Mr Chow.

The Principal looked shocked. 'He's coming here. Now? Couldn't we meet him on neutral ground?'

Mr Chow's tone changed to one of reassurance. 'Miriam, you needn't worry. He won't bite you, you know.'

The Principal continued to look annoyed but she quickly changed the subject. 'You know Bridget is quite like her father but we're making progress with her.'

Bridget breathed in sharply. The Principal and Mr Chow shivered and looked quickly around the room. Bridget had to get her breathing under control.

'That's good. We wouldn't want another Patrick although she has created that wonderful website. *Howlo* is amazing. She is very much the networker.'

'Just like her dad,' Principal Goode added sarcastically. 'Though I'm sure he set up *Howlo* for a reason.'

Bridget felt confused. What did Mr Chow mean when he said that they wouldn't like her to turn out like her Dad? If she were visible, her cheeks would be burning red.

'But tell me, did Mr Boyle receive the consignment of 'vamp-form' I sent last month?'

The Principal huffed. 'Yes, we did receive it. I don't see why we have to have it here. No one in this school wants to take something that turns them into a vampire, you know.'

Mr Chow rotated his purple eye towards the Principal. 'Miriam, you must always have a supply of it to protect yourselves. Anyway, the transformation lasts only a few hours. It's a security measure. Just make sure none of your students get their hands on it.'

Bridget sniffed and the Principal and Mr Chow turned to look in her direction. She needed to control herself.

Suddenly, there was a loud rap on the window and the Principal rolled her eyes. 'Doesn't he ever enter by the door?'

The Principal got up to open the window. Mr Chow chided her good humouredly. 'We all have our differences, Miriam.'

Bridget watched as a tall man wearing a long black coat flew in the open window. The cool air from outside followed him in and the blind flapped noisily. He practically knocked over the computer screen as he hovered over the desk and the Principal tut-tutted in annoyance.

After the Principal had closed the window, the man steadied himself and stood up straight. Bridget watched as he carefully flattened the lapels of his coat.

'Professor, it is so good to see you,' said Mr Chow cheerily. 'Please sit down.'

Bridget could see that the Principal was most uncomfortable having a vampire in the room. The Professor was terribly elegant with greying, slicked-back hair, cherry-red lips and crystal clear eyes full of utter contempt for Principal Goode.

Mr Chow observed the interaction. It was clear neither one of them was prepared to start the conversation. 'I'm sure, Professor, that you have some questions for the Principal.'

The Professor looked sideways at Mr Chow and spoke, his voice was calm, his tone icy. 'Do you have a description of the Dracul students you claim were in Mallow Castle?

The Principal seemed shocked. She glanced at Mr Chow and gritted her teeth. 'Yes,' she said coldly eyeing her notes from the night before. 'There was a vampire named Molly, a male vampire from New York called Willy and Vlad, a Russian footballer.'

'I understand they stopped one of your students from being killed by another,' the Professor said snugly as he scribbled in his notebook.

The Principal's face turned red. 'If you already knew which of your students were in the park last night, why ask me for a description?'

The Professor gave the Principal a look of disdain. 'I'm just checking the facts – students do lie.' He flicked back the pages of his notebook. 'Fortunately for you though, my students saved this Bridget, '

'Well, so Bridget says anyway,' answered the Principal coolly. 'Though I can't understand why your vampires would want to protect a werewolf.'

The Professor simply shrugged and then glanced coldly from the Principal to Mr Chow. The Professor's mouth curled down in condescension and Bridget knew he was picking up her scent.

'Yes, well, I've been thinking about this overnight,' said Mr Chow. 'I've just presided over a very serious dispute between the skin crawlers and the eye gougers. You remember them?'

The Principal grimaced, 'Not those groups with the eczema and the bloody eyes.'

'Exactly, Principal. They've been fighting for years but we've got a resolution now and they've become friends. Isn't it obvious that Molly and her friends are trying to move the werewolf-vampire conflict on? We should build on this incident using a new approach,' said Mr Chow.

'What do you mean?' asked the Principal.

Mr Chow waved a tentacle, 'I think we should encourage friendly interaction between Herr Wolf's werewolves and Dracul's vampires.'

The Principal and Professor were reduced to silence.

Mr Chow continued in a whispery tone, waving his tentacle fingers back and forth. 'For centuries, there has been too much bloodshed during the fierce battles between your two tribes. Maybe it's time for a change, a different perspective, a mutual respect.'

'I'm not sure what you're proposing, Mr Chow,' said the Professor curtly fiddling with his bow tie.

Mr Chow's pale-pink tentacles entwined around one another turning his hands into two large plaits. 'Why don't we see if you can find common ground? We'll organise one or two social events and bring students of the two schools together.'

The Principal tugged at her hair and snorted. 'What... like a dance?'

'Maybe a boat race or a quiz night? They are all young teenagers. I'm sure they have more in common than we think.' His tentacles lost their braiding and waved about again.

Bridget's heart hopped in her chest with excitement.

The Professor remained silent, appearing lost in thought. He frowned when he realised that Mr Chow and Principal Goode were looking directly at him, waiting for a response. 'Whatever are you suggesting?' he said, taking a sharp intake of fake breath.

'I'm suggesting that you no longer discriminate against each other. Haven't you been fighting for centuries? Isn't it time for a change?' Mr Chow stared at them both. No one spoke. 'So, what about organising a boat race for next Sunday morning to start us off?' He stabbed his left tentacle on the table to indicate that this suggestion was not something that could be refused.

'My students participating in a boat race with... werewolves?' hissed the Professor.

'Well, why not? It will reduce the tension among your students if we make an announcement today. I'm sure they're expecting to be expelled.' Mr Chow looked at the Principal and the Professor. The look of distress on both their faces conveyed their feelings perfectly.

'It's a huge departure for me too. The idea that my students could develop friendships with...yours,' said the Principal, looking angrily at the Professor.

Bridget wanted to shout out. 'Yes, let's all be friends,' but naturally she stopped herself.

After a brief, silent stand-off, Mr Chow rapped his tentacles on the desk. The Principal and the Professor didn't look at all convinced but they both nodded in agreement.

Mr Chow smiled. 'We can look forward to an exciting boat race on Sunday.' There was deathly silence in the room. 'Just one last thing. I would like to document this momentous occasion by inviting the journalists on *Idiotic News* to write an article and take photographs of the race, for the werewolf social networking website *Howlo.*'

He focused his attention on the Professor. 'Bridget, the student who was saved last night, is a founding member of the site and I think it would be a good idea to post a report on the race. It *is* historic after all.'

Bridget almost yelled with delight. She'd always wanted to meet Leona and Issey from *Idiotic News*.

'But the presenters of *Idiotic News* are humans,' said the Professor haughtily.

Mr Chow sucked his lip. 'Yes, but they are ex-sanatorium patients. They're already considered daft. No rational person ever believes their stories. As a matter of fact, their programme is broadcast into the rooms of every mental home in China.'

The Principal nodded slowly. 'And in Ireland too. I suppose we could invite them here, Mr Chow.'

The Professor rolled his eyes but nodded his head in agreement.

Bridget's stomach rumbled gently and everyone turned around. If she didn't get out of the room quickly, she'd be discovered. What could she do? She rushed over to the window and pulled back the latch, the window flew open with a gale of wind, scattering papers all over floor. While the Principal tried to shut the window, Bridget opened the door and ran out into the hall, her heart pounding.

She dashed over to where the camera couldn't see her and watched as her hands began to reappear. So close!

Bridget heard Mr Chow ask the Professor to fly up to the dam and put a mild sedative in the drinking water to make sure that the locals slept late on Sunday. A shadow appeared in the doorway. Bridget held her breath as the Principal banged the door shut.

***

'I want you to be captain,' the Principal said to Bridget.

Bridget looked at the others. All of them were stunned about the impending boat race and Eddie began to snarl.

'The race *is* happening, students. Mr Chow has decided. There is no discussion. I have no intention of losing and you all need to work closely with your captain.'

Even though Bridget knew that the announcement was coming, she still felt hugely excited. She'd love to have told Katy everything but knew she couldn't. Bridget hadn't erased the tape of her going into the Principal's room and it worried her that she might still be found out but hopefully no one would examine the tapes closely. She could get expelled and that thought scared her. How strange?

Earlier today, Bridget had so desperately wanted to leave rehab but that was before she listened in at the meeting. Bridget realised that she'd never discover about her father and about why the teachers were so negative about him unless she stayed.

The Principal cleared her throat. 'One more thing, I'm insisting that everyone shape shifts the night before the race. It will give us a competitive advantage. I'll let you hunt the night before to sate your appetites. And I, for one, look forward to wiping the condescending sneer off the Professor's face when we beat those snobby vampires.'

Bridget protested loudly. 'But why do we need to shape shift?'

The Principal looked at Bridget with a degree of irritation. 'This is in the interests of the school Bridget. You'll have to put your discomfort about being a wolf aside for the sake of your team.'

Bridget puffed her cheeks out as Katy came over and put her arm around her. 'Bridget, you get to be captain. It'll be so much fun.'

As the Principal turned to leave she looked over. 'Bridget, a word please.'

Bridget followed the Principal down the corridor and into her office. The Principal slapped her hand on her desk. 'Bridget, while I appreciate you're progress in rehab is slow and you are reluctant to metamorphose into a wolf, I will not tolerate being undermined by you. I am the Principal of this school and if I decide that you are shape shifting on Saturday evening then that is what you are doing. Is that understood?'

Bridget's face reddened. She hadn't expected the Principal to be so sharp with her. Bridget's lips quivered and tears fell on her cheeks. 'I...I'm sorry. It won't happen again.'

The Principal looked on unsympathetically and handed Bridget a tissue. 'From now on, I need you to participate in two 'embrace your inner wolf' classes a day, okay?'

'I can't...' protested Bridget.

'You can and you will,' said the Principal sourly.

Bridget nodded and continued to dab her eyes with the tissue.

'Is there anything you want to talk about?' asked the Principal coldly.

'No,' said Bridget as she continued to sniffle.

'Let's put this incident behind us then.'

Bridget shoulders slouched as she left the office. Two inner wolf classes a day – how could she bear it? For the first time, she realised that the Principal had other motives than helping her. She didn't care about Bridget's feelings at all. She just wanted her to conform. This made Bridget even more determined to find out more about her father and about what the WEEsistance were up to.

***

'I've done a little background check on your new friend, Katy,' Mary said to Bridget via Skype.

'What?' Bridget answered tetchily.

'There's no need for that tone, Pidge. She's from a very violent family, you know. They've been in trouble with the law a lot. I'm not sure she's the sort of person you should be associating with.'

'Mum, the only reason I'm still here is because of Katy. She talked me into staying.'

'I'm only trying to protect you, Pidge.' Mary hesitated. 'Although I suppose if she's encouraging you to stay at Herr Wolf's then that's good.'

***

The night before the race, after an especially difficult shape shift for Bridget, she sat in the study and surveyed a few of her pack with pride. Katy was a fantastic horsewoman with a magnificent stroke. All six and a half feet of Roald, dressed in his long blond coat, were muscles in marvellous motion. Andrew, although short, had strong powerful arms and legs. Miguel's work rate was exceptional even though his chest rattled constantly. Simonetta couldn't participate because her weight was still low, but she insisted on helping with the snacks after the race. Even though it was going to be junk snacks, Bridget felt Simonetta needed as much encouragement as possible.

Bridget walked over to Andrew. 'How is your incontinence today?' she whispered.

'Not good Bridget,' he said sadly. Bridget knew that Andrew had been hoping to play an important role on the team. I'm sorry about this, Andrew. I hope you understand. I need the strongest team and I...'

'Don't worry, Bridget.' Andrew said patting Bridget's fur.

'Okay,' said Bridget turning to Saori. 'Do you want to be part of the team?'

Saori almost scratched her ears off with delight and she ran over to Bridget to celebrate.

Eddie looked on crossly. 'And what about me? You've chosen that flea-bitten Jap before me!'

Everyone stared at Eddie in disgust. Bridget's eyes flashed. 'We can't rely on your temperament, Eddie. Lose the attitude and maybe you'll get picked next time! Oh, and apologise to Saori.'

Bridget felt proud of herself. She'd actually stood up to Eddie. Being the team captain had definitely helped her confidence. Eddie seethed and sulked off, followed by Katy. Bridget watched as Katy tilted her head towards Eddie's chest and rubbed his back. This irritated Bridget though she told herself that as his sponsor, Katy was obliged to pretend to care.

'I'm a little nervous, chaps,' said Andrew, adjusting the stop watch that Bridget had given him to take charge of.

Bridget yawned. 'Don't worry, Andrew. We'll beat the vampires, stop watch or not. The rules say that they can't fly and we know they're not as strong as us. I think we should go to bed early though. We need all our strength for tomorrow.'

Dev wanted to discuss more tactics. 'If we get off to a good start, they won't have a hope of catching us,' he said enthusiastically.

'Let's get a good night's sleep,' said Roald, licking his very hairy left paw.

'Bed, everyone,' yelled Bridget. They growled in agreement and headed to the dormitories. Before long, the building shook with the sounds of thunderous snoring.

Bridget lay awake, thinking about meeting the vampires and *Idiotic News* and she hugged her knees to her chest with excitement.

9

THE BOAT RACE

Bridget waited on the river bank and looked around at her team. Werewolves of various hair colours and body shapes were taking up position, stretching, growling and pouncing in the early morning light. Bridget smiled and sauntered over to Roald and Andrew for a chat. Then she looked across at the vampires and sighed.

Groups of vampires with their translucent skin and red lips hurried down to the river. Some flew to save time while others trundled down the grassy bank with tissues covering their noses because the stench from the river was so strong. Bridget saw some baby bats chirping their heads off, flying behind. What a cliché: vampires with their bats.

The river was narrow and it was easy to overhear the vampires' conversations. Bridget bent down and pretended to undo the ropes on her boat but was listening intently.

'Do we have a decision yet?' snapped a posh-sounding English girl with wavy hair and penetrating green eyes. 'A captain...anyone. The race *is* in one hour.'

'Annabel, can't we decide just before the race?' said a squat, German-sounding boy as he adjusted his team hat.

Everyone agreed noisily. Bridget saw Molly arrive with a box of bottles. Molly looked over at Bridget and grinned. Bridget waved her paw shyly and then looked down at the rope knot she was pretending to tie. 'Hey Bridget,' whispered two voices. Bridget looked up to see Vlad and

Willy grinning over at her and she smiled back at them. They had to be the friendliest vampires ever!

Molly began talking. 'The Professor said we have to drink regular Blud. We need the full calorie content.' Bridget watched as Molly pulled the cap off a bottle of cranberry juice.

Then Bridget noticed the Professor in the distance, pouring anti-Godwin's formula into the river. The haze of wretched odour slowly evaporated, taking the awful smell with it. Bridget let out a sigh of relief.

Over the crackling loudspeaker a shrill voice that Bridget didn't recognise called out. 'Attention all students,' – the speaker cleared their throat and continued - 'Attention all students. The inaugural boat race between Dracul's College and Herr Wolf's Institute will begin shortly.'

The sound of scratching coming from the microphone made everyone on the river bank hiss and moan. 'Can all participants please take their places beside their boats as the race starts in five minutes?'

All of a sudden, the microphone screeched as it clearly hit the floor and a collective chuckle lightened the tense atmosphere. Bridget looked over at the vampires again and smirked. She was really looking forward to beating them.

Principal Goode approached Bridget. 'Bridget, this is Leona Coco and Issey Nolo,' she said condescendingly

Bridget looked at the two girls. Leona wore a purple tartan suit and had bright orange hair while Issey was dressed in a leopard-print coat with green wellington boots underneath. They looked like they sounded on their radio programme – loopy.

Bridget rushed at them, throwing her hairy paws around their shoulders. 'Oh, I'm so happy to finally meet you. How are you?'

Leona pressed her body against Bridget's fur and laughed loudly. 'Bridget, *furry* nice to meet you after all this time! Ha, ha. Did you get the joke there?' Bridget giggled back. Issey just looked down at the grass and kicked a tuft of it.

Katy, Andrew and Roald came over for the introductions but the Principal interrupted them all. 'Hurry, the race is starting. You can talk to Leona and Issey later.'

Bridget gestured to her team to take up their positions on the boat and she plonked herself down. Katy sat opposite her. Roald and Dev sat behind her, with Miguel and Saori positioned at the end. Andrew came over with his stop watch and patted Bridget on the shoulder. 'Good luck team!'

'I hope they beat you,' snarled Eddie as he turned and walked back up the river bank.

While Dev and Roald shouted at him in anger, Bridget rolled her eyes and bellowed to her team, 'Forget about Eddie. Concentrate on the race now, everyone.'

Principal Goode tottered down the river bank in sky-scraper heels. She caught Miguel sniggering at her. 'Ra-bou-tin,' she said, gesturing to her shoes, 'made from the best rabbit skin.' She straightened herself up. 'Team Herr Wolf, we need to win and that's what you're going to do.'

Bridget and the others cheered and whistled. Miss Joyce and the choir took their places and howled the victory song.

'Herr Wolf's the best and we'll beat the rest,
A-whooo, A-whooo,
We've got the brawn though its early morn,
A-whoo, A-whoo,
We'll trounce Dracul's cos we're really cool,
A-whoo, A-whoo,
We'll bring home the cup and we'll act like wups,
A-whoo, A-whoo, A-whoooo!

The singing stopped and the wolves shouted, 'go, wolves!' wiggling their tails in the direction of the Dracul's team. The vampires responded to them by hissing.

Now, it was the vampires' turn to show off. A fat bat took position overhead. She let out a little squeak and a bunch of smaller bats flew together over the crowds. Their tiny wings extended and contracted, little bat feet standing on the shoulders of other bats as they formed the words, 'Dracul's to win!' one letter at a time. The spectators spelled the words and grinned. It was a spectacular show. The bats were adorable and Bridget wanted to coo at them but stopped herself when she saw Eddie sneering angrily at her. The bats finished with an exclamation mark and both teams lifted their oars.

The shrill voice sounded once again over the tannoy, 'Can all rowers go to the starting line please?'

The Professor rushed over to the vampires. 'Have you decided on your leader?' he snapped.

'No,' they replied in an exhausted moan.

'Right then, I will have to decide for you.' The Professor looked around. 'Werner, take your place at the helm of the boat!'

Werner looked shocked and noisy chatter erupted from the vampire group.

'I will have no disagreement. Werner is your new team leader and you must follow his commands!' thundered the Professor.

'But Professor,' pleaded Annabel, 'his stuttering gets worse when he's under pressure.'

The Professor could not be swayed. 'Decision made. Now take your places on the boat, oars at the ready.'

Bridget, who'd been watching intently, almost squealed out loud. 'I've heard it all now, a vampire with a stutter!' she muttered to Katy. Katy sniggered and stared over at Werner.

Werner looked as if he'd been slapped in the face with a wet fish and the boat hadn't even left the shore. He glanced nervously at his team-mates. They glared back which only made his face go bright scarlet. 'My f...f...f...f...fellow t...t...t...eam m...m...m...mates.'

'Oh for flip sake, we can't listen to this! The race will be over by the time he finishes his motivational speech,' Annabel snarled.

'Shhh,' said Willy and they all turned to look at Werner again who was busy straightening himself up.

Annabel snorted. 'Werner, you'll have to avoid the letters, b c, e, f, h, i, j, k, l, m, n, o, p, q, r, s, t, u, v, w, x, y ... Stick to g, d and a.'

Werner looked at Annabel, nodded and simply said. 'Go Dracul's!'

**

Bridget and her team rowed to the starting line which consisted of two strips of white paint that had been applied to the grass from the top of the bank down to the water's edge on either side.

'On your marks... get set... GO!'

The Institute pulled away first, the large muscles on Bridget's hairy upper arms rippled as she plunged her oar into the water, forward and then backwards with a far more incredible power than she could ever manage as a human. 'Come on Team Wolf,' she cried.

Roald and Dev were well matched. Roald's breathing was steady as he rowed. 'Must concentrate,' Roald said, his pink tongue hanging onto his chest.

'Mi-guellll,' drawled Katy, 'Be an angel and keep an eye on your left there and let me know if you see any of those blood sucking critters coming up beside us.'

'No problemo.'

After about thirty seconds, Bridget cried. 'We're in the lead, keep it up.'

The vampires were finding the race much more stressful. An anxious Werner could only pronounce three letters without his stutter. He yelled, 'Advance Dracul's,' 'Demolish,' and 'Galvanise,' over and over.

His team looked confused: Annabel was unhappy with their start and shouted. 'Captain, they've made fantastic ground. We need to put more effort in.'

Willy was using his broad shoulders to power the oars into the water. 'Come on peeps, we've got to win,' he shouted enthusiastically.

Molly, who was normally very twitchy, had settled down well and hadn't moved from position once.

'Double activity,' shouted Werner.

Soon the vampires got into a rhythm and speeded up their rowing, forward, back, forward, back. With every stroke they sounded like small trains as their oars hit the water. The baby bats flew overhead, chirping encouragement.

'Good,' shouted Werner. They were slowly catching up on the wolves.

Bridget shouted to her team. 'Guys, they've doubled their efforts and are closing the gap. Row faster! Come on everyone, we've got to beat them.'

'A-whoooo,' Herr Wolf's team howled in agreement.

This sudden acceleration brought the werewolves to the half-way point first but, as they steered their boat around the buoy that floated in the centre of the river, they could see the vampires advancing fast, hissing and booing as they approached. A bell rang from the shore and everyone cheered.

The wolves turned the boat and cheered with panting voices. So strenuous was their effort that the fur on their heads stuck flat to their skin and drops of sweat fell from their ears.

Katy looked like she was starting to tire so Bridget shouted, 'Come on Katy. Give it some oooomph!'

Katy grinned, her lovely white fangs glistening in the early morning sun. 'Y'all are doin' fine, bless your hearts.'

On Dracul's boat however, the rowers looked exhausted and when they turned at the half-way mark, they were still three lengths behind the wolves. Annabel looked on in dismay. 'We'll never catch them,' she said downheartedly, 'they're just too strong for us.'

Werner repeated his limited commands over and over, droning on from the top of the boat. 'Advance! Gather Ground! Dominate!'

Once past the half way mark, the vampires increased the speed of their strokes and caught up slightly. But Bridget and the wolves were still three lengths ahead, and the finishing line beckoned in the distance.

'It's hopeless,' yelled Annabel, 'we haven't a chance of catching them. They've already won.'

Suddenly Horst, who'd been completely silent throughout the race, whispered hoarsly. 'I have a solution. You know, my farts just might save the day for us. I could release some methane now, if you wish?'

'But that would be cheating,' said Molly sneakily.

'We've got to win,' shouted Willy and Annabel together. They all looked at their captain. Werner hesitated for a moment and then nodded his head in agreement.

'Wunderbar. One über fart coming up,' said Horst as he positioned his posterior over to one side of the boat. He was careful to clear the top. The boat jolted and propelled forward, although not fast enough to attract suspicion.

'Fantastic,' shouted Annabel. 'One more should do it, Horst.'

Horst concentrated again, his mouth forming and sounding a little 'O'. This time the boat glided forward and now the vampires were almost level with the werewolves.

Bridget turned in disbelief when she saw the vampires closing in on them. She screamed at Roald and Dev, 'Come on, they've caught up on us. Row FASTER!'

With the force of Horst's wind, the vampire's boat had become unstable. Annabel shouted, 'Quickly Willy, move over to the right side to give us ballast.' Willy shifted into position. As the boat stabilised, the vampires surged ahead of Bridget and her bewildered team-mates. All Bridget could do was growl. The crowds on the river banks screamed, losing all reason with the excitement.

Roald yelled hysterically at the others. 'If we lose this race, I'll have to tie my tongue in for a week!'

But Bridget wasn't going to give up. She'd worked far too hard for this. She might be intrigued by Molly and the other vampires, but there was no way she was going to let them win. 'Go wolves,' she shouted over and over. She and the wolves fought back courageously, driving their oars deeper into the choppy water.

The vampires looked across at Bridget and her team as a spray of water splashed their faces and they flashed their gleaming teeth in defiance.

'Go Dracul's,' shouted Werner, his voice ragged and torn.

Bridget roared out. 'Come on everyone, one last effort! We can do it!'

The vampires hissed and drove their oars harder still racing slightly ahead of the wolves. The wolves countered and closed the gap. The vampires dug again in unison and nudged ahead. The screaming spectators couldn't contain themselves and Andrew played 'We are the champions' from the river bank.

Finally, with one last effort, the vampires inched over the line to loud sounds of cheering and howling.

Bridget and the wolves leaned over their oars, panting with exhaustion and glowering at each other. Exasperated, Roald shouted. 'What happened, Bridget? How come they passed us out? We were so far ahead?'

Bridget looked over at the vampires and growled. She watched angrily as Annabel stood up on the boat and kissed Werner full on the mouth. 'We did it! We did it!' she screamed.

Everyone hugged the overwhelmed German boy all at once. 'Horst, you're our saviour, thanks so much,' they shouted, showering him with hugs and kisses.

Watching them celebrate, Bridget's temper began to rise. She didn't care what the vampires thought of her now – she was with her team, Herr Wolf's. 'The vampires cheated. They couldn't have caught up with us otherwise. They're cheaters.'

Molly, Vlad and Willy looked at Bridget and scowled. Eddie jeered from the side and Roald and Dev growled at him to shut up. Bridget called over Principal Goode, who was standing close by looking furious.

'Principal Goode, we wish to make a complaint,' Bridget said trying to control her temper by digging her paws into the fur on her thighs.

The Principal tiptoed over to the side of the boat and spoke angrily. 'It was just incredible. They were so far behind you and then suddenly you were neck and neck. I simply don't understand it. I will make a formal complaint to Mr Chow and Professor Prosperus,' she said, struggling to stop herself from falling into the boat.

The Principal eyed the vampires with suspicion. Professor Prosperus was standing congratulating everyone as a clearly irritated Principal approached Dracul's boat. 'Professor Prosperus, could I have a word with you privately,' she said gesturing to the bridge she'd just walked across.

'Certainly, Principal Goode,' his triumphant smile slowly fading. Mr Chow crept over to join them too.

Principal Goode placed her hands on her stomach and adjusted her tone. 'Professor Prosperus, something very irregular occurred during that race. There is no possible way that your team could have beaten us given that we were a clear three lengths ahead in the last hundred metres.'

The Professor ran one of his long nails through his hair in an agitated manner. 'I'm not sure what you're suggesting Principal Goode but I can assure you that no flying occurred during the race.'

Mr Chow interrupted them. 'Allow me to intervene. Perhaps we could discuss this in a more *private* setting.'

10

Winners and Losers

Bridget watched the interaction between the Principal, Mr Chow and the Professor. She looked across at Molly and Molly looked away. Vlad and Willy wouldn't even make eye contact with Bridget. It didn't feel right. They'd been so friendly before the race. Bridget noticed that even after all their exertions, the vampires looked exactly the same: no redness or sweating – nothing at all. Bridget's team continued to jeer and howl and Roald pounced off the boat in defiance.

Mr Chow addressed the crowd. 'Please everyone, can we all take a minute to reflect?' he pleaded, pressing one of his tentacles against the microphone.

Everyone stood and stared and waited. It was a tense moment until the girls from *Idiotic News* approached Mr Chow. 'We took the liberty of taping the whole race, Mr Chow,' said Leona Coco quickly.

'It's all here,' continued Issey Nolo, tapping on the video recorder she held in her hand.

Mr Chow looked solemn as he took the recorder from Issey. 'That's most helpful of you, thank you.' He placed the loudspeaker to his face and spoke carefully. 'There appears to be disagreement over the result of the boat race. I suggest both team captains come with us to the boat house to investigate this further.'

Bridget led her team in an explosion of whistles and felt a rush of adrenalin. Katy, Roald and Dev patted her fur as she walked over to Mr Chow's side. Werner joined them, his piercing, nervous eyes flashing as he hung his head a little.

Mr Chow looked around him and wagged a tentacle, 'We are retiring to the boat house where we will view some film evidence, given to us by the journalists from *Idiotic News*. We will return soon with a decision. Mrs Joyce from the Institute and Nano Burke from Dracul's are in charge during our absence. If anyone starts a fight, they face immediate expulsion. Thank you.' He switched the microphone off.

The spectators huddled together as the small group made their way to the boat house.

Once the review team assembled, Bridget looked over at Werner. When he extended his hand to her, she felt oddly conflicted and she left him hanging.

'I'm V-v-v-erner,' he stammered.

Bridget looked at his blond hair and yellow-brown eyes. She wanted to ask him where he was from but, under the circumstances, it seemed silly to ask.

Mr Chow placed the camcorder on a table and pressed the 'ON' button. The light flickered and suddenly they could see the two teams lining up. Leona had positioned the camera on a tripod in the middle of the bridge, so the images were clear and steady. Bridget watched with a surge of pride as the wolves turned the central buoy. It was clear that they were at least three lengths ahead. Then something very strange happened. Within ten seconds the vampires were almost level with the wolves.

'Stop the tape,' said Principal Goode. 'There's something very irregular here.'

Mr Chow rewound, zoomed in on the vampires and slowed the tape down. The Professor shifted in his chair, looking uncomfortable. What they saw was Horst moving in his seat and raising his posterior above the side of the boat.

'What *is* he doing?' asked Principal Goode. The film showed that just after Horst moved, the boat accelerated a lot. It was clear Horst was the reason for the increase in speed. Werner cleared his throat nervously and looked down.

'Why did Horst come to Dracul's, Professor?' asked Mr Chow.

'Severe flatulence,' replied the Professor, his eyes blinking with embarrassment.

Bridget and the Principal gasped as it instantly dawned on them how exactly the race had been won. Everyone looked accusingly at Werner and he peered out the window. Mr Chow spoke first. 'It appears Dracul's won the race as a consequence of Horst's farts. Would everyone agree with this?'

'Absolutely,' said Principal Goode, angrily. 'He cheated.'

Bridget looked across at a guilty-looking Werner and felt a little sorry for him.

The Professor glared at Werner and sniffed in anger. 'Yes,' he admitted, 'it's clear that Dracul's team cheated.'

'I propose that we declare Herr Wolf's Institute outright winners,' said Mr Chow.

'Agreed,' said Principal Goode and the Professor in unison.

***

The Principal ushered Bridget ahead of her as she walked back to the boats with Mr Chow. The Professor walked behind them, Werner trailing at the back.

'Principal Goode, I feel it is important for me to announce the result. We don't want to inflame the situation further,' Mr Chow insisted.

'Oh, but there must be an apology,' Principal Goode protested.

'Yes,' said the Professor, curtly, 'I will make the apology.'

The casual chatter of the crowd quietened when Bridget, Mr Chow, the Principal, the Professor and Werner approached on the river bank.

'Having viewed the tape, we declare Herr Wolf's Institute the winners of the race,' said Mr Chow.

A thunderous growl went up from the assembled wolves. Bridget raced over to Katy, Roald, Dev, Miguel and Saori and they all jumped up and down hugging each other. Miguel howled with great force and he chuckled, delighted with himself. Simonetta and Andrew ran over to the boat and gave everyone another hug. Eddie gave his usual 'Eddie sneer.'

The spectator vampires booed and hissed. The Professor spoke next, his voice tense. 'It seems our team cheated during the race.'

The booing now came from Bridget and her team. Through gritted teeth, the Professor continued, 'I apologise on behalf of Dracul's. There will be sanctions for this behaviour and we are very disappointed with our students. I ask Dracul College students to applaud the rightful winners, Herr Wolf's Institute!'

Werner went back to his whispering team who all looked over at Bridget. Vlad and Willy joined in a congratulatory shout and Annabel gave them a filthy look. With his paw, Eddie made a large L shape for losers and gestured at the vampires. Seeing this, the head bat and all the baby bats released bat droppings onto Eddie's head. Eddie swiped at the bats in annoyance as the little pellets stuck to his fur. Bridget looked around her with pride. She glanced over at Molly and Molly mouthed 'Sorry.'

Principal Goode took the microphone roughly from the Professor. 'Congratulations to the Institute for winning fair and square. We are so proud of you today.'

Mr Chow added. 'I propose that we run a quiz next weekend. The College and the Institute will have a chance to compete again.'

The Principal and Professor began to object but Mr Chow touched their arms. 'Everyone, finish up your drinks. We need to leave in ten minutes.'

**

Bridget watched as a furious-looking Annabel marched after Leona and Issey as they walked off. Bridget felt there might be trouble so she immediately followed them.

'I must say, I'm very pleased with myself Issey,' Leona said proudly. 'This is a bit of a journalistic coup, you know. It's definitely the best day of our lives. I thought interviewing talking cats and dogs about their insecurities and tea towels about tips on how to remove water stains was monumental but today's events are truly historic.'

Issey nodded. 'I can see us being presented with the Pulitzer Prize Leona. I really can.'

They eyed each other sneakily while Leona removed something from her inside pocket. Then Leona began speaking in a whisper. 'This is Leona Coco reporting directly from the scene of the inaugural boat race between Herr Wolf's Institute and Dracul's College...'

Suddenly Leona looked up to see Annabel glaring down at her.

'What do you think you're doing?' Annabel shouted, her pale green eyes narrowing.

'N...nothing,' replied Leona nervously. Annabel bent over Leona so fast that she didn't even see her take the dicta phone she'd been holding and fling it into the river.

'W...what did you do that for?' shouted Leona, her expensive recording device now destroyed.

'You are not authorised to make any recordings post-event, you stupid tadpole,' shouted Annabel.

Leona started to cry. 'She didn't mean anything by it. We're journalists, you know. Our job is to capture the moment,' pleaded Issey.

'Journalists,' sneered Annabel, 'more like lunatics!'

Annabel leaned forward into a pounce pose and began to hiss. Both Leona and Issey shut their eyes, as if they expected to be killed any minute. Bridget was just about to jump onto Annabel when Bridget heard a dull plop.

Everyone looked down and saw a set of dentures on the grass. Annabel went bright red. Bridget started to giggle – a vampire with false teeth. Annabel turned around to Bridget, an awkward look in her eyes.

Leona looked at Issey and said dryly. 'How was she going to kill us, gum us to death?'

Great peals of laughter shook Leona and Issey's bodies, convulsions reaching their limbs and their mouths yawning in hysterical laughter. Bridget held the side of her fur and laughed too. Annabel caught Bridget's eye as she leaned down to pick up her teeth. Bridget smiled at her and Annabel looked nervously back. Molly came over and jerkily patted Annabel on the shoulder. 'The werewolves have problems too, you know, Annabel.'

Bridget walked back over to her team and relayed the joke. 'They're even bigger losers than us,' said Roald, not even trying to contain his guffaws. Annabel stared over at Bridget with a humiliated look. Bridget momentarily felt guilty but then something very strange caught her eye - Eddie was starting up a conversation with Vlad (who was just waking up from a nap). Bridget approached cautiously.

'You said you're in the Kiska league, mate?' said Eddie. Bridget was shocked at Eddie's friendly tone.

'Da. You play also?' replied Vlad.

'Not professionally. I did trials a month ago. I'm a massive Chelsea supporter.'

'Da, Chelsea. I would love to play for them,' said Vlad wiping the sleep from his eyes. 'My favourite player is

Cech,' he continued enthusiastically. He sat up on the grass and Eddie lay down near him.

'Yeah, he's not bad but Drogba is better. Did you see that game against Liverpool last month?' Eddie didn't wait for an answer, 'Superb football...a hat trick in one afternoon.'

Bridget looked across at Katy. She too was watching Eddie's interaction with Vlad but Katy was scowling and making fists of her paws. It was as if Katy was waiting for something to happen. Then Katy's eyes flickered onto Bridget's face and her expression changed to a grin. Confused, Bridget smiled back. Perhaps she'd had a row with Eddie or was worried that he might attack Vlad? When Bridget thought about that, she realised it was definitely time for them to leave. 'Let's go everyone,' Bridget shouted.

Eddie glared at Bridget. His talons were extended, like he was getting ready to fight. If that happened, anybody could have been killed. Eddie moved away from Vlad's side and walked slowly over to his class mates.

Katy rushed up to Bridget. 'Thank goodness you called time! I was so worried that Eddie was going to start a riot.'

'I think he was, Katy.' Bridget looked around her. 'I just need to say goodbye to Leona and Issey. You go ahead.'

Bridget waved at Leona and tried to find Molly but saw, to her disappointment, that most of the vampires had already left. Could she really be friends with these vampires? It seemed like that was all she wanted to do.

11

The Quiz

Even though Bridget had been forced to shape shift on Wednesday, she hadn't thought about leaving the Institute once. And she knew why - she wanted to meet the vampires again. 'I'm really excited to see the inside of Dracul's,' she said excitedly to Katy as they got ready to go to leave the Institute.

This would be the first time the vampires would see Bridget in human form and she was ecstatic. She wondered why their good opinion mattered so much to her. She envied them the fact that they weren't animals and she knew she looked a lot better as a human.

'Is everybody ready?' shouted Lou from the corridor. 'It's raining so we're bussing over.'

Bridget and Katy rushed downstairs to join the others. Roald was wearing a plaited necklace of pink-white garlic bulbs and everyone sniggered at him. 'You can't be too careful,' he laughed.

'They're not afraid of garlic. They just hate the smell of it,' said Bridget.

'How do you know?' asked Andrew.

'I looked it up on the internet. I think the only thing that kills them is us and fire.

'I'll bring my lighter then,' Roald guffawed.

The bus whipped up the roads of Mallow making its way to the sign for Dracul's. The entrance to the castle had a wonderful sweeping, tree-lined driveway. When the bus moved up the drive, the speed made gravel and dust rise up like vapour blocking the view out the windows. They could just about make out the main door with Dracul's impressive crest of black and yellow hanging from a silver disc. As the bus came to an abrupt stop, small bats circled overhead. Seconds later, they flew in rotation forming a cross. Bridget giggled.

A chilly mist hovered over the entrance door and seeing this, Roald said 'Whooo!' in a spooky voice.

As they walked into Dracul's entrance hall, Bridget's mouth dropped open. The school was pristine, not a cobweb, paw mark or piece of straw in sight. There wasn't even a smell, just marbled floors and wood panelling as far as her eyes could see. They walked through heavy wooden doors covered in delicate cross emblems.

'Thought they hated crosses,' said Katy under her breath.

'They don't. It's just another made up myth about them,' answered Bridget, taking the whole impressive scene in with her eyes.

In the imposing assembly hall, the high ceilings echoed with noise from the dragging chairs from the floor below and a large stage held two enormous tables placed at an angle. In the centre, a temporary podium had been erected. The Principal, the Professor and Mr Chow sat silently in front of the stage around a small rectangular table.

Simonetta and Roald designed a large banner that hung grandly from two long steel poles. The Institute's logo of a howling white wolf on a green background contrasted sharply with the Dracul's logo of a yellow letter D set against black.

'Nice banner,' said Bridget to Simonetta.

Molly came out towards them and everyone except Bridget seemed to bristle. 'Welcome, can you come with me backstage?' she asked, her limbs twitching.

'Of course,' said Bridget and everyone followed her and Molly.

It had been decided, in the interests of fairness, that the presenters of *Idiotic News* would set the questions and that Leona would compère round one followed by Issey in round two.

'This is for Bridget,' Leona said handing Saori a plastic cup with steaming liquid inside. 'It's hot chocolate.'

***

Five minutes later, Leona walked purposefully on to the stage to the sound of loud cheering and hissing. She was wearing a bright pink dress with a purple polka-dot headscarf and red-rimmed glasses.

Leona grinned and shouted. 'Welcome to the inaugural Dracul's College versus Herr Wolf's Institute Quiz.' She then gestured to Issey at the side of the stage and the theme music of *Idiotic News* started. Bridget poked her head out from behind the curtain and giggled. She knew the tune and began to sing along:

'Id-iotic News, Id-iotic News,
you list-en to stup-id re-views

Id-iotic News, Id-iotic News ,
you lis-ten to stup-id re-views
We interview talk-ing cats and dogs and ham-sters too
And the best part is that you don't have to be smart
To listen to Id-iotic News
Id-iotic News, Id-iotic News,
you listen to stup-id re-views
Id-iotic News, Id-iotic News ,
you listen to stup-id reviews'

When the song finished, everyone clapped and cheered. 'What a brilliant song,' chuckled Roald. The excitement was building. Team Herr Wolf approached their table first. With Bridget again chosen as leader, she bounced forward.

'First up, for the Institute...Bridget from Dublin.' A huge whistle went up.

'Go, Bridget!' shouted Katy from the side.

Bridget waved and sat down.

Miguel approached with confidence, his brawny arms swinging by his sides.

'Next up, it's Miguel from Spain.'

'Hola!' he hollered.

'Next up, we have Simonetta from Milan.'

Simonetta walked on stage adjusting her sunglasses. 'Ciao, Ciao,' she shouted.

'Roald from Amsterdam.'

'Hoi,' shouted Roald as he sloped on to the stage, his tongue lolling about practically washing his face.

'Andrew from Oxford.' Andrew left a trail of urine at the side of the stage and shouted, 'Cheers' as he plonked himself down.

'Dev from Mumbai.'

'Hey,' shouted Dev, taking a sniff from his inhaler.

'Saori from Tokyo.' Saori bowed to the audience.

'And finally Katy from Tennessee.'

Katy screamed her thanks. 'Yee haw, bless your hearts.'

Bridget looked out at the audience and all she could see were intimidating vampire eyes blazing back at her. The cheering continued as Leona started talking again.

'Introducing Dracul's College team captain, Willy from New York.'

'NYC in da house!' Willy jumped up on to the stage to loud cheers.

Annabel bounced forward, smiling her gummy smile. The vampires hissed and snarled in appreciation. 'Jolly good,' shouted Annabel, waving at everyone.

'Next up, it's Horst from Frankfurt.'

'Wie gehts,' shouted Horst, adjusting his flatulence belt. The cheering continued.

'Molly from Galway.' Molly flew on stage, waving and fidgeting with her hair.

Leona was clearly thrilled with the response to her intros.

'Privyet,' shouted Vlad from the audience, then he quickly fell off his chair, snoring.

Eddie ran his tongue along his teeth and Bridget cringed. Was he planning to cause trouble during the quiz? Katy had suggested excluding him from the team because she was worried that he might start a fight. When Bridget looked down at him now, she wasn't sure she'd made the right decision. Eddie had been furious when Bridget told him that he wouldn't be part of the quiz. 'Exclusion is a form of bullying, mate,' he'd protested loudly. One thing Eddie knew all about was bullying.

Over the din, Leona told the contestants to take their seats. Everyone rushed to sit down, their seats making a loud clatter on the floor as they pulled them in.

Bridget looked across at the vampires and saw them all staring earnestly back at her and her team, taking in their human forms. Bridget heard Annabel mutter nastily under her breath. 'They're just animals in human clothing.' The condescension hurt Bridget, but Molly smiled back and that calmed Bridget down.

'The rules are simple. I ask individual questions to each team for two points. If the individual cannot answer the question, it is then opened up to the whole team. If the team can't answer the question, it is passed over to the other team for one point. If anyone from the audience shouts the answer, their team will lose a point. Is that clear, teams?'

'Yes,' they shouted in unison.

'Okay, the Institute won the toss.' The vampires hissed a little. 'We'll start with the Institute.' The volume of howling and snarling increased until the Professor stood up and looked around sternly, quietening the room.

Leona flashed her impish grin. 'Bridget, as team captain you will start. For two points, can you tell me, what is the opposite of cauliflower?'

Bridget looked stunned, eyeing the others nervously and hoping that one of them had the answer. But all of them looked confused. Team vampire looked surprised at the question too but remained silent. Bridget put her hands up to her face and pulled at a tuft of hair.

'Do you want to pass it to the other members of your team?' asked a smirking Leona. Miguel nodded and the team huddled together.

'What is caul – i – flower?' whispered Simonetta.

'It's a vegetable,' said Saori.

'But there can't be an opposite to a cauliflower?' Roald said looking perplexed.

'For me, in this moment, it makes no sense,' said Miguel.

Leona coughed. 'Institute, we must have your answer please.'

'Sorry...we don't know,' said Bridget sadly.

Leona continued to smirk. 'For one point, Dracul's, what is the opposite of cauliflower?' The vampires moved so close together they were almost rubbing shoulders, but Bridget picked up their whispers. Annabel looked bewildered. 'I've never heard a question like this before,' she said.

'Maybe its flowery-col,' said Molly. Willy and Werner looked at her, unconvinced but shrugging. 'What do we have to lose?'

Annabel's tone was tentative, 'Is it flowery-col?'

'No!' said Leona. Everyone waited eagerly for the answer. 'It's broccoli,' Leona snorted in a fit of giggles.

The audience started to laugh and both teams stared in disbelief. The Principal, the Professor and Mr Chow shifted in their seats uneasily.

Leona grinned and began again. 'For Dracul's College.' A surge of pride swept through the hall and all the vamps stood up on their tippy toes and showed their dazzling white fangs. 'If guilty is the opposite of innocent, then what is the opposite of woah?'

Annabel answered quickly and clearly, 'Happiness.' Annabel supposed that happiness could be the opposite of woe, but she still didn't understand the purpose of the questions.

Molly, Willy and Horst waited.

'No,' said Leona proudly. 'It's giddy up.'

A few nervous titters ran around the assembly hall after which a roar of laughter went up as everyone made the connection between the word 'Woah' and 'Giddy up,' both ways to tell a horse to stop and to move. Roald gave Bridget a lick on her cheek, so happy that the vampires hadn't scored a point.

'Don't crow too soon,' said Bridget, frowning as she wiped Roald's saliva off her face. She looked over at Horst and caught the most dreadful smell.

Around them, the hall was full of chuckling and jeering and Annabel looked angrily at Willy.

The Professor nudged Mr Chow and whispered, 'I think allowing *Idiotic News* to set the questions has been a truly idiotic idea.' Mr Chow looked back at the Professor uncomfortably.

Saori took a sip of hot chocolate and Katy tugged at her arm. 'That's Bridget's drink, you know.'

Saori reddened. 'I'm sorry, Katy. I am very thirsty. You think Bridget will mind?'

Katy was about to answer her when Leona started again. 'Simonetta, what sort of memory does a horse's computer have?'

Simonetta looked at Leona and the rest of her team in puzzlement. 'Horses don't have computers, do they?' she said looking at a bamboozled Bridget. What an idiotic quiz! When it was clear that Simonetta did not have a response, Leona motioned to the rest of the team. 'Anyone, team Herr Wolf's?'

'No,' they replied together.

'Dracul's, for one point?' she asked.

Molly, Horst and Willy looked at each other and realised that no one had the answer. 'No,' said Annabel reluctantly.

'The answer is giddy bytes,' said Leona.

Another explosion of laughter came from the audience but this time the teams looked angry. The Principal and the Professor looked at each other tensely and Mr Chow rolled his purple eye, just as the Professor got up and left the room. Leona tried to continue with her questions, although some jeering had started in the hall.

Suddenly, the fire alarm rang. The intense noise made vampires and werewolves screech and howl in agony and everyone cleared the hall in record time. Leona looked around her in dismay. The quiz had been a disaster.

***

Outside, Bridget was keen to start a conversation with the vampires but she didn't know how to make the first move. She smiled hopefully over at Molly. Annabel scowled back at Bridget. After a few uncertain moments, Molly flew over to Bridget's group. "That was the craziest quiz I've ever been at,' she said fidgeting with her hair and laughing.

Bridget grinned back. 'Yeah. It was.'

Molly peered into Bridget's face. 'You look so different tonight, Bridget. Does it hurt when you change?'

Bridget smiled shyly. 'Yes it hurts, but only for a few minutes.'

Andrew tugged at his trousers and began talking to Willy who had just walked over. 'Why did you come to Dracul's, Willy?'

Willy chuckled, 'I need a blood transfusion.'

Bridget and the other werewolves tittered. They *really* were a weird bunch of vampires.

'Why are you in rehab?' Willy said looking at Bridget and Andrew.

Andrew clutched at the front of his trousers. 'Out of control territory marking tendencies.'

Willy whooped with laughter and Annabel wrinkled her nose as she came closer.

'I don't like changing into a werewolf,' Bridget said quietly.

'Oh, really,' said Molly with a look of surprise.

'It's the body stuff I don't like. The smells...'

Annabel interrupted. 'Yes, it must be terrible being a stinking animal.'

Bridget looked away anxiously and Molly gave Annabel a filthy look.

'Attention everyone. I've just spoken to Mr Finnegan and although there's no evidence of a fire, he's insisting, in the interest of safety, that we call off the quiz for tonight,' said the Professor stiffly as he walked towards the students.

Bridget felt let down. She was eager to talk more to Molly. There were shouts of disappointment from the others. Molly, Annabel and Willy wandered back to their classmates. Leona and Issey, who had just come outside, looked crushed by the news.

'It's a disaster Bridget,' Leona said when Bridget went over to comfort her.

The Professor clapped his hands together. 'We would like to thank Idiotic News for all their efforts. I'll be in touch shortly to re-arrange another night.'

Bridget spotted Eddie with a nasty grin on his face, circling the crowd. She hoped he wasn't going to start a fight.

'I don't feel very well,' said Saori clutching her stomach.

The Principal looked at Saori, sniffed and raised her voice. 'Can all Herr Wolf's staff and students please make their way to the bus now?'

As they moved off, Bridget waved over at Molly, Willy, and Vlad and they waved back. Bridget's heart thumped in her chest. She liked them, really liked them. She looked around for Katy and saw her walking ahead with Eddie. How could Katy stand Eddie's company?

As they got to the bus, Saori grasped Simonetta's arm and began to moan. 'Ow, Ow, Ow!'

'Quickly, help Saori into the bus. We need to bring her to the infirmary right away,' said the Principal.

Andrew and Roald lifted Saori onto the seat of the bus. For the whole of the short journey back, Saori wriggled around in her seat, groaning in pain and turning an alarming shade of green.

12

DEATH IN THE INSTITUTE

Bridget woke to the sound of raised voices and footsteps running up and down the corridor outside her room. Shifting on the straw, she watched as Katy and Simonetta sat up.

'What's wrong?' said Bridget rubbing her eyes.

Katy shrugged but Bridget could tell that she was worried.

There was a rap on the door. 'Bridget, Katy, Simonetta, come down stairs quickly. Something's happened,' a tense sounding Andrew said.

They all dressed quickly and hurried down to the common room to find Roald, Andrew, Miguel, Dev and Eddie already waiting at the door.

Bridget looked over at Katy. 'I wonder what's up?'

Katy just shrugged but appeared ill at ease.

Looking around the common room, it was clear that something dreadful had happened. The Principal was comforting Lou and Mr Boyle was blowing his nose with a handkerchief. His hands trembled and when he took his glasses off, it was obvious that he'd been crying. Mr Chow crept around the group of teachers, seeming to offer reassurance.

Principal Goode looked up when she saw Bridget coming. Her hair was untidy and her eyes red. 'Sit down everyone. We have some dreadful news.' She looked sideways at Mr Boyle and he nodded his head.

'I'm not sure how to tell you this but a terrible thing has happened...' The Principal's voice started to break and Bridget felt her heart tighten a little in her chest. 'Saori died last night.'

An audible gasp ran around the room. Bridget closed her eyes and opened them again. How could poor sweet Saori be dead? Katy grabbed onto Bridget's arm and started to sob. Simonetta slumped down and covered her hand with her mouth. Bridget looked across at the boys. They were all staring ahead, collectively shaking their heads. Eddie sat immobile.

'I know it's a terrible shock for you all,' said the Principal looking over at Lou Flanagan as she let out a massive sob. Mr Boyle quickly put his arm around Lou's shoulder in comfort.

Bridget heard a sob and realised it had escaped from her own mouth. She felt a crushing weight on her chest - like the moment she'd heard that her father had died.

'But that's not the worst of it. We're ninety nine per cent certain that Saori was poisoned.'

Bridget looked around at the others again. Simonetta had burst into tears and Roald and Andrew hugged her in comfort.

'Mr Boyle found traces of anti-freeze in Saori's stomach.'

'Anti-freeze,' said an astonished looking Roald. 'But how could that be?'

Mr Boyle took over the conversation. 'This is what I don't understand. We've had plenty of lessons about the dangers of anti-freeze. You've all been sniffing it for weeks. I made so sure everyone could identify the smell because it's the most dangerous poison to us.' His voice became quieter, 'but for some reason, Saori swallowed some.'

The Principal patted his shoulder. 'Please don't blame yourself, Mr Boyle. We will get to the bottom of this mystery.' Then the Principal straightened herself up and her tone changed to a harsher one. 'Saori couldn't have consumed anything here with anti-freeze in it, but who knows what she could have gotten her hands on at Dracul's? Did any of you see her drink anything?'

'Maybe the vampires poisoned her?' Eddie said with a sneer.

Mr Chow answered slowly. 'We've already checked with them. The Professor insists that they only have frozen blood in the college and Saori wouldn't have drunk that.'

'I saw Saori drinking hot chocolate when the quiz was on. Leona gave it to her,' Katy offered.

'Are you sure, Katy?' asked the Principal, her eyes widening.

Katy nodded. 'Yeah, I was right beside her.'

The Principal stared steadily at Mr Boyle. 'We need to phone Leona immediately. We'll be back in a few minutes.'

The teachers hurried out and Bridget looked around the room. Miguel looked like he might cry at any moment. Roald still had his arms wrapped around Simonetta's shaking body. Dev touched his inhaler with a shaky hand and even Eddie looked sad. Katy continued to cry on Bridget's shoulder and her tears wet the material on Bridget's collar. Bridget tried vainly to swallow a lump in her throat but tears soon ran down her face and she couldn't stop trembling.

'I can't believe it...' said Simonetta in between sobs. 'Poor Saori.'

A few minutes later, the door swung open and the Principal, her face contorted in anger, walked back in followed by all the teachers. Everyone hushed up immediately.

'Leona says she can't remember much. She remembers seeing a card with Bridget's name on it beside a cup of hot chocolate. She gave the drink to Saori for Bridget.' The Principal didn't look at all convinced. 'Well that's what she says anyway.'

'But Leona isn't exactly a reliable source now, is she? I mean she poisoned a teacher in her old school and got locked up for it,' Mr Boyle blurted out.

Bridget couldn't believe what they were saying. Poor Leona was getting the blame for Saori's death. 'The story about the poisoned teacher was made up. Leona wouldn't hurt a fly, you all know that. There's got to be another explanation...' Bridget protested looking around at everyone.

The Principal interrupted Bridget tetchily. 'That's enough, Bridget.' Then she turned to Mr Boyle. 'I will phone the Professor to see if he can find the note or the cup. Couldn't you do finger print analysis?'

Mr Boyle's face looked hopeful. 'Yes I could. Excellent idea.'

The Principal began to rush out of the room, but hesitated before she reached the door. 'Until we find the cup, no one is to talk to Leona. Is that clear?' She looked directly at Bridget and Bridget felt her face colour even more.

After the Principal left, Bridget realised that all the others were looking nervously at her. 'What?' she said anxiously.

'According to Leona, *you* were the real target,' said Roald.

Bridget hadn't thought about that at all and she let out a gasp. 'But, but Leona wouldn't hurt me. Can't you see there's been a mistake?' Bridget pleaded.

'Leona's mad, Bridget,' Eddie snapped.

Bridget started to protest again but none of the others wanted to listen to her. She couldn't believe how quickly they'd forgotten about poor Saori when there was a poisoning and Leona to gossip about. Bridget had to get out of the room. Racing into the hallway and up the stairs into the dormitory, she fell in a heap on the hay and let her tears overtake her.

***

Half an hour later, Bridget's laptop beeped and she saw her mother's ID appear.

'Paddy just told me the news. Are you alright, Pidge?'

'I can't believe that Saori is gone.' Bridget's voice cracked a little.

'But Leona may have tried to kill you Bridget. I'm so worried. You must never again associate with her.'

'Mum, Leona didn't do this.' Bridget swiped her damp eyes with the back of her hand.

'How can you be sure?'

'I just know Leona. She couldn't do this, she's innocent.'

'Well, you're not to talk to her until they find out, okay? I suggested to Principal Goode that I'd drive over to see you today but she says that's not necessary. What do you think?'

'Mum, I'm fine. Don't come here. Everything will be fine. I'll phone you back in a few hours.'

***

Classes were suspended as a mark of respect to Saori, and everyone congregated around the computer and clicked into *Howlo*. For hours, they watched the slide shows and mini movies that they'd put up over the last few weeks. Saori appeared in most of them. Everyone, but Eddie, cried their eyes out when they saw Saori chatting and dancing. There was even film of her singing 'Born to Be Wild' in her unusual high-pitched voice. And when it came to night time, everyone fell into bed, exhausted.

Only Bridget couldn't sleep. Saori was gone forever and Bridget couldn't stop thinking about poor Leona and the distress she must be going through. But maybe Leona had interfered with the drink? Bridget desperately needed to talk to her. She'd tried listening to *Idiotic News* earlier but the announcer said that the programme had been cancelled and Leona and Issey's mobiles were switched off. But another thing bothered Bridget, Principal Goode hadn't seen remotely upset that Bridget could've been poisoned. If only they found the cup. One thing was for sure, finding the cup was the only way to discover the truth.

13

A Werewolf Transformed

'Yeah, the reception is better out here Sharon... it's been terrible, yes, we still can't believe it...' Bridget paused and gulped some air. 'I don't want to think about the quiz because Saori, you know, was poisoned then,' Bridget tried to control her voice. 'But they're trying to find the cup that she drank from. It's still an open investigation. I've been posting updates on *Howlo* and I'm very worried about Leona. I still can't get through to her. Can you let me know if she makes contact with anyone?'

Bridget was on her mobile outside the front entrance to the Institute. Over the last few days, it'd been easier to get out of shape shifting because everyone was still so upset. Bridget hadn't actually thought of leaving the Institute once.

Bridget started walking back inside when she heard a rustle. She looked up at the trees and her heart almost stopped. Vlad's face smirked down at her. She let out a full breath when she saw Molly and Willy hidden in the branches beside him.

Molly flitted from branch to branch, whispering. 'We've come to see how you are. We were sorry to hear about your friend Saori.'

Bridget's body had gone rigid with the initial fright. But something more important weighed on her mind. Even though she was delighted to see them again, she couldn't ignore the fact that she was outnumbered by three able vampires. Her pulse raced – she'd been warned over the years never to be alone with more than one at any time.

Bridget smiled back at Molly, but responded cautiously. 'You'll have to forgive me, Molly but because there are three of you I'd feel much safer with a friend or two out here.'

Molly nodded. 'Katy and Roald are very friendly. Hang on a minute,' Bridget said dashing inside.

Bridget returned with Katy and Roald. Katy had a huge grin on her face and Roald's tongue licked his face involuntarily. Molly giggled.

'Why don't y'all come down from the trees?' said Katy, her tone welcoming.

Vlad and Willy dropped down and Molly stayed on the lowest branch. Vlad shuddered into a yawn and Molly fidgeted with her fingers. They all looked uncomfortable and no one seemed to know what to say next.

'You're taking a big risk crossing the river again,' Bridget said betraying her admiration.

'Oh, I know,' said Molly smirking. 'But we couldn't help ourselves. We needed to see how you all are after the death and everything.'

Somehow, Bridget instinctively trusted the truth of Molly's compassion. 'Thank you. We're still very sad about Saori.'

'The Professor made us scour the grounds of the college for the cup. Unfortunately, we couldn't find it,' said Molly apologetically.

'Please keep looking. You know, poor Leona is being blamed. If we could only find the cup,' Bridget sounded sad again.

Bridget looked over at Katy and Roald. Katy now appeared oddly tense and it looked like Roald didn't really believe that the vampires were genuinely interested in Saori's death. Vampires were killing machines and ordinarily a werewolf's death wouldn't be important to them. But these vampires were different. They had to be.

Bridget was relieved when Katy changed the subject. 'Andrew told us you're rap name is Willy Pee,' she said looking at Willy. 'What's the 'p' stand for?'

Willy chuckled. 'I'm pale Willy on account of my anaemia so everyone calls me Willy Pee for short.'

Bridget and Katy laughed nervously. 'Why are you in Dracul's?' Bridget asked Molly.

Molly wrapped a lock of hair around her finger. 'I'm in re-vamp because I've got VADD. I'm here to be calmed down.'

'VADD?'

'Yeah, vampire attention deficit disorder.'

Bridget laughed out loud, 'that's crazy. Why are your nails shorter on those fingers?' she said pointing at Molly's hands.

'I'm a chronic nail biter. I'm allowed to bite these two nails though,' Molly said waving her fingers.

Roald leaned forward and licked Molly's nails with his tongue and everyone squealed in disgust. Molly flinched then frowned. 'I thought it might tickle. I'd love to feel tickled again.'

Bridget looked in shock at Molly's longing face. It wasn't all fun being a vampire after all because you never got to feel anything. 'You said re-vamp?' asked Bridget.

'Yeah, we're in rehab just like you guys are. Our rehab is called revamp,' said Molly banging her ankles off the branch of the tree.

'I heard you talking about downloading pictures on to some site,' Molly continued. 'What site is that?'

'Oh it's *Howlo*. It's the werewolf social networking site. I set it up actually and now it's got eight thousand members worldwide. You've got your own site?'

'No, vampires are kind of anti-social,' replied Molly hopelessly.

'Well, it's easy to set one up. I could help you if you like.'

Katy drummed the side of the tree with her fingers impatiently and from time to time, she turned and looked back towards the windows.

'And you know, Willy, if you set up a vampire site, you could upload some raps for it. It would be cool,' Bridget continued encouragingly.

'I'm down with that,' replied Willy with a smile.

Feeling more secure, the werewolves and vampires moved closer together. Katy continued to sneak peeks back inside while Bridget, Molly and Vlad talked about *Howlo*. Bridget knew that she shouldn't but she ended up asking Molly for her telephone number.

A moment later, Bridget heard Eddie shouting for Katy. Bridget's body tensed and the vampires flew back up to the trees. Bridget looked up nervously at Molly and whispered,

'You'd better go now. You've seen what Eddie is like. Thanks for coming over.'

'Y'all have a safe trip home,' said Katy.

'Thank peeps. We'll see you soon,' said Willy.

As Bridget walked back inside, she had to admit she was sad to see Molly go.

***

As the vampires flew back to the college, Vlad became sleepy. He fell into a deep doze dropping out of the sky and landing leadenly on to a glistening moonlit field. Molly and Willy continued to the college without him. Later in the night, as the moon beamed down, Vlad snored gently on the grass.

Slowly, a small creature approached Vlad's heaving body and looked down at his ivory-coloured face. Cocking its crooked head, the creature hesitated a moment before kneeling down beside Vlad. It lifted up Vlad's right arm and examined it, gently stroking the long pointed nails at the end of Vlad's fingers. Then pulling up Vlad's sleeve to expose his deathly pale skin, a set of jagged teeth chomped down on Vlad's arm as he continued to snore.

***

Bridget woke to the sound of her phone ringing. She ran outside and took the call.

'Bridget?'

'Yes.'

'It's Molly here.'

'Oh Molly. I'm surprised to hear from you so soon. What's up?' Bridget looked around the corridor to make sure that no one was about.

'Something happened to Vlad on the way home last night. He fell asleep in a field.' Molly relayed the story in breathless gasps. 'Anyway, we left him there but this morning, he's behaving really weird. He's in the canteen talking gibberish and dancing jigs. I know this is going to sound crazy, but you don't think he's been bitten by a leprechaun, do you?'

Bridget gasped and put her hand to her mouth. 'Actually, yes. We've been warned to stay away from the fairy fort. Do you remember if there were little stones arranged in a large circle in this field?'

'Yeah, I wondered what those were.'

'Those stones mark the fairy fort and once you go inside their boundaries, you're in the leprechauns' territory. And with Vlad asleep he was an easy target.'

'What can we do?' Molly wondered. 'If we have to explain this to the Professor, he'll know we sneaked out again and this time we *will* be expelled.'

Bridget hesitated. In the distance, the Principal was walking towards her and Bridget ducked into the study to avoid her. 'There is an antidote. Mr Boyle, our science teacher has developed it. The only problem is, it's under lock and key in our lab. I'd have to steal it and that would be dangerous. I'll call you back after I've spoken to Katy. Give me half an hour. Okay?'

Bridget hung up and ran back into the dormitory. Katy looked up at Bridget mid-stretch on the hay. Simonetta was still asleep. 'Get dressed. I need to talk to you. Meet me outside the lab in five minutes.'

***

Bridget rushed out of the lab to find Katy coming down the stairs. Looking up at the cameras, she ushered Katy down the corridor.

'What's wrong, Bridget?' asked Katy with a look of worry on her face.

When they were out of sight of the cameras, Bridget said. 'The vampires need our help.'

'What?' said Katy looking utterly shocked.

'Molly just phoned. Vlad was bitten by a leprechaun last night. I've just stolen the formula from Mr Boyle's room and I'm going over to the college with it now.'

'What? Are you nuts, Bridget? You can't just go over there. They're a bunch of vampires, you'll get yourself...' Katy stopped and inhaled, 'killed.'

'I have to do it. They'll get expelled if I don't. And besides I can have a look for Saori's cup when I'm over there. I know I'll do a better job of searching for it than the vampires. I'm positive that Leona isn't responsible for poisoning Saori.'

Katy looked distressed. 'You really are fascinated by those vampires, aren't you? But how will you get into the college without being seen?'

'I've found a way. I can't tell you because I don't want to implicate you too. But please cover for me this morning with the Principal. I'll meet you at the bridge at lunchtime.'

Katy continued to argue for several minutes, but eventually she gave in. Bridget's mind was resolved.

***

Bridget felt so afraid about what she was about to do. She ran out the front door, onto the grass. When she was close to the river, she stopped and phoned Molly. 'I'm coming over now with the antidote,' she said, almost out of breath.

Molly sounded frightened. 'But you can't come here. They'll pick your scent up a mile off.'

'Don't worry Molly. I won't be coming as a werewolf. Meet me at the back of the castle in ten minutes.'

Bridget looked at the two bottles in her hand. She was about to do something incredibly dangerous. Her heart raced with fear but then she remembered what Mr Chow had said about the effect only lasting a few hours. She opened the lid of the violet bottle and swallowed a mouthful of the mixture. It tasted like she'd sucked a lemon. She struck her tongue out and shuddered.

Sitting on the grass, Bridget waited for something to happen. Suddenly, her vision blurred. It felt like the atmosphere around her was fizzy – as if she was inside a bottle of soft drink and everything was bubbly. The taste of lemon lessened.

Bridget saw her skin go whiter and felt the most incredible thing – her heart began to slow down, slower and slower and slower until it stopped completely! No sound came from her body at all. Looking down, she saw that her nails had grown long and pointy. She knew she was gasping when she looked down at them but she couldn't feel the air entering her lungs. Her chest no longer moved because her body had stopped breathing. She was temporarily dead. Bridget had transformed herself into a vampire.

Bridget got up and ran forward, putting her hands out in front of her – like Superman would. She laughed loudly, but her rib cage didn't move at all. She flew up in the air, over trees, screaming. She didn't feel excited or happy. There was no heat in her body at all and even though she could hear the wind whizzing past her ears and see her trousers flapping in the breeze, she couldn't feel anything. It was the weirdest feeling - without feeling - ever.

Bridget swerved to her left and then she saw Molly below. Molly had her back to Bridget as she swooped onto the path. Wait until she sees me! 'Molly,' she whispered.

Molly turned around and squinted. 'Bridget. Oh. What have you done?'

Bridget giggled. 'I'm a vampire...well, 'til lunchtime anyway.'

'But how...?' Molly's mouth dropped open.

'I can't tell you how I did it.' She pointed at her pocket. 'But I've brought the antidote for Vlad. We'll need to administer it carefully. Can we go inside?'

Molly looked so flummoxed, she couldn't speak. She just kept staring.

'I'll give him two dozes before lunchtime and then you can take over. And Molly, would you please stop staring at me?'

'I'm sorry Bridget but it's just so unbelievable. I can't get my head around you being a vampire.' Molly wrung her hands together. 'Okay, Vlad's in the canteen. I'll tell everyone that you're my cousin.'

***

Inside, Vlad skipped towards Willy and Annabel. He turned when he saw Molly and Bridget walk in. Bridget inhaled some fake breath.

'Da, top of the mornin' to ya' Molly. And who is your lovely friend?' Vlad asked in a lilting voice.

Molly twitched. 'Oh everyone, this is...Martha, my cousin. She just called to drop something off...'

Annabel nodded coolly, studying Bridget's face carefully.

'What up, homey? Are you a loser like us?' asked Willy.

'Stop saying that,' hissed Annabel crossly.

'Welcome there, Martha,' tittered Vlad. 'A lovely female specimen you are too.'

Bridget laughed nervously. None of the vampires recognised her. She must look quite different. She wished she could look in the mirror, but she might not have been able to see her reflection even if she could.

Vlad interrupted her thoughts. 'I'm only after getting meself out of the bed this instant and I've a cracking headache but a thirst for whiskey and dancing.' Then he started to dance a jig while singing in an Irish lilt.

'Tour-ah, lour-ah, lour-ah, tou-rah, lour-ah- lee, tour-ah lour-ah lou-rah, Dracul's the on-ly place for me!'

As Vlad continued jigging about, right over to a large dispensing machine, Molly and Willy burst out laughing.

'What's that?' Bridget asked Molly in amazement.

'It's our fridge,' said Molly.

Bridget looked at this huge vending machine with its rows of glass bottles, containing red liquid.

'It's blood,' said Molly tapping the machine.

Bridget examined the rows and saw that there were three types of bottles, a red-and-green one called *Blud,* a red-and-blue called *Blud Liet* and a red-and-black called *Blud Extra.* To use the refrigerator, the vampires had to type in their own personal code.

'Don't they sell cold blood at your school?' asked Annabel curiously.

'No,' stammered Bridget. She thought the vampires only drank warm blood straight out of a human's neck.

'I find the *Blud extra* gives me gas,' laughed Willy. 'We definitely keep that away from Horst.' Everyone giggled and Horst waved over when he saw them all looking at him.

'Willy, me ould flow-er, would you care to join me for a tincture of whiskey over on the fairy fort where we might spy a rainbow and find our crock of gold?' said Vlad.

Everyone laughed at Vlad's antics but Bridget was more interested in watching Vlad drink. To her surprise, Vlad took out a *Blud* and gulped it all down in one go.

'What is the matter with him this morning? He's acting most strangely,' Annabel asked Molly.

'Oh, Willy and I have a bet with him that he can't act like a leprechaun. How's he doing?'

'Oh really,' Annabel laughed for the first time. 'Must say he's hilarious, especially with the Russian accent.'

Molly moved Willy to one side and whispered. 'We've got the antidote. Follow us up to the dormitory with Vlad.'

Molly pressed a button in the vending machine and a bottle of *Blud* released itself and clunked down the chute. Then she escorted Bridget out of the canteen.

***

When they got into the dormitory, Bridget looked around in amazement. Five coffins sat in the corner and Bridget let out a shriek. 'Coffins! I thought that was just make believe.'

'Oh, we don't sleep much but we keep them for the sake of tradition.'

Bridget squinted and walked over to a coffin with white paint. Inside it was a large pink duvet with tiny hearts embroidered on the edges. 'This is so cute,' she said running her hand along the top of it.

'That's mine,' said Molly proudly.

Bridget caught a glimpse of herself in the mirror. 'Oh, I do have a reflection! I don't look anything like me.' She touched her face and admired her pale, flawless skin and crystal clear eyes.

Willy cleared his throat as he came into the dormitory. 'Yo, how did your cousin get her hands on the anti-dote?' Molly smiled nervously at Bridget.

'I'm not her cousin. It's me...Bridget.'

14

THE CUP

Willy's mouth gaped and Vlad jigged around in circles chattering. 'Is it yourself there, Bridget? You're looking very pale, right enough.'

At that moment, Annabel burst through the door. 'I knew it. I knew there was something familiar about her,' she narrowed her eyes and sneered. 'How did you do it?'

'I drank something but it's only temporary,' Bridget explained. 'I'm here to help you with Vlad. The leprechaunitis antidote is very tricky.'

Annabel continued to glare at Bridget, and Molly looked at Annabel impatiently. 'Look Annabel. Vlad got bitten by a leprechaun last night. Bridget has the antidote here. She's trying to make sure we don't get expelled, okay?'

'When did all this happen? And how come you're only telling me about it now?' said Annabel, looking hurt.

'We snuck out again last night. Bridget's gone out on a limb to help us.'

Annabel said nothing but continued to stare as Bridget took two bottles out of her pocket. 'A spoon anyone?' Bridget asked.

Willy rushed over and Molly handed Bridget the open bottle of *Blud*.

'I still can't believe there's cold blood in there?' said Bridget grimacing.

Molly smirked, 'Aren't you thirsty for it now?'

Bridget blinked and shuddered, 'Actually, I only like the taste of blood when I'm in wolf form and I certainly don't feel like drinking it now.'

All the vampires laughed nervously. 'And we thought we had problems,' said Willy.

Bridget quickly poured a few drops of the antidote from the green bottle and mixed it with a few drops from the blue bottle. Then she dipped the spoon in the bottle of *Blud* and gave it a stir. 'It's two drops of blue and two drops of green twice a day for the first two days and after that, he'll only need a drop of each. I'll give him a second dose just before I leave at lunchtime.'

Annabel handed the *Blud* to Vlad and he gulped it down greedily. Then he slumped on a coffin and fell asleep. Molly sighed with relief and grabbed the bottles of antidote, putting them up on a shelf. 'I'll stay up here and give him his second doze when he wakes up,' said Bridget.

'Thanks Bridget. We'll be forever in your debt. I'll come back up at twelve,' said Molly looking at Willy and Annabel.

'Let's go,' said Annabel giving Bridget a half-hearted smile.

'Willy,' Nano's voice shouted from the corridor outside. Bridget looked at Molly and Annabel and placed her hand over her mouth.

'Yes,' said Willy.

'What's going on? Why are you not at class?' said Nano.

Willy ran out to the corridor. 'Sorry Nano. Vlad's fallen asleep so I was just putting him in his coffin.'

Nano's voice sounded stern. 'Who's with you?' she asked as she charged into the dormitory. Molly stepped forward. 'This is my cousin Martha. She's visiting for the morning.'

Nano sniffed and regarded Bridget coldly. 'We don't normally allow strangers into the school but as she's your cousin I'm sure the Professor will have no problem.' Nano looked away from Bridget and glared at the others. 'Now hurry down to class.'

Bridget didn't move and Nano said, 'You're hardly going to sit up here with the snore master all morning.' She pointed at Vlad, 'come along to class with the others.'

Bridget scowled but Molly smirked at her. 'Our first class is in the Eye Clinic. It'll be fine.'

After walking along endless spotlessly clean, odourless corridors, they came to the Clinic. On the wall outside, a photo chart of every student hung. Bridget spotted Molly's photo. 'How come your picture is all fuzzy?'

'Oh, I couldn't stay still long enough for the camera to focus,' giggled Molly.

The interior of the room was fantastically modern with stainless steel walls and plush moss green leather seating. There were eight seats in front of a wall of floor to ceiling mirrors. Bridget knew she had to be careful not to stare too much but she couldn't help herself. Annabel looked in the mirror and adjusted her lenses with her finger. 'That's better,' she muttered. Everyone settled down in their chairs and waited.

A tall blonde vampire with a curious left eye walked to the front of the room. Molly leaned over and whispered. 'That's Penny Lopey.'

Penny's eye looked like glass: pale blue and egg-shaped. Bridget looked at all the certificates on the wall. One or two were from the International Institute of Vampire Dental Practice but most of them were awards which had been presented to Penny from the 'Dracula Comedy Association.' Bridget counted twenty four certificates. 'Hello Martha, welcome to our class. Nano has told me that you're visiting today.'

Bridget winked at Molly. Werner, Suzy and Horst looked over at Bridget and stared awkwardly. Bridget wondered if they recognised her.

'Yes... let's start with a quick eye test.'

Penny pointed to a sign, similar to a standard eye test for humans, displaying a chart of letters which started with a large typeface working down to smaller print. There was a difference between the standard chart and this one though. This one used only one word – all the way down.

Miss Lopey moved over to Horst and Horst farted a little, releasing a toxic stench. Miss Lopey grimaced and took out a handkerchief. Placing it over her mouth, she spluttered. 'Horst, begin and be quick.'

Bridget began to laugh and looked over at Molly for her reaction. Molly twitched on her seat, clearly having great difficulty keeping still.

Horst had excellent vision but he farted throughout his reading and Annabel looked on in disgust. 'B L O...toot...O

D...toot...D B L...toot O O...toot...D...toot...toot...' Horst adjusted himself on the seat and released more wind.

'Just read the bottom line please Horst. Hurry!' cried Miss Lopey, pressing her handkerchief to her face.

'L O O D B L O O D B,' yelled Horst in his clipped German tones, holding on to his air until the last 'B' whereupon he farted with such force that he blew his chair back twenty feet. Everyone rushed over to the window but Bridget sat still. She had lost her sense of smell entirely – how fortunate was that!

Miss Lopey's bad eye watered and she gulped asking Annabel to open the window and Horst to stand beside it. Meanwhile, Molly could no longer stay still and flew around the room. 'Molly, please sit down and start your eye test,' pleaded Miss Lopey.

Bridget looked up at Molly and giggled because Molly looked like an oversized bee, flying in circles above their heads.

'I'll do my best to sit, Miss Lopey, but as you know, I'm very hyper. I may have to hover during class.'

Molly sat down again, but within two seconds she was up, hovering over the chair. The others glanced at her easily. They were all used to Molly flying about.

Molly began to read the chart. 'B L...' She tried to sit again but her limbs twitched with nervous tension, 'Em...O...O.' Soon she was up again with a magnificent swish, flying all the way to the ceiling.

Miss Lopey took out her notes again. 'Molly, please stop. We will have to alter your diet as we can't continue to have this whizzing around during class. You'll give us all whiplash.'

Werner was very nervous starting his test, 'B B B B ...L L L .....O O O........O O O ...D D D ...'he stammered, taking forever to pronounce each letter.

Annabel looked impatiently out the window, Molly flew near the ceiling and Horst farted. Bridget smirked. She'd imagined that the vampires were perfect, but instead this group was a bigger bunch of no-hopers than the students in the Institute. She couldn't wait to tell Katy all about them.

Miss Lopey nodded at Willy. Willy looked around at the others and grinned, 'Let me break it down for you, B to the L to the O to the O!'

Everyone hissed and laughed and even Miss Lopey smiled.

'O to the D to the B to the L...'

Bridget tapped the desk with her new nails and Annabel moved her hips in time to the rhythm. Molly followed the beat and flew in formation and Horst farted in time. Soon the whole class was chuckling and giggling.

A loud scratch noise sounded, like nails running down a blackboard, and they walked out into the corridor.

'Next is flying practice,' Molly whispered to Bridget.

Bridget beamed back at her. She would enjoy this. The flying instructor, Edmund Burke was a sinister-looking vampire with incredibly long limbs. His teeth were slightly crooked and he had a small hunch in his back as though his body had succumbed to the weight of his limbs. Outside, they were surrounded by a small forest with stunning sycamore trees.

'When we're close to the trees, the smell from the river is not as strong,' Molly explained to Bridget. Mr Burke turned to face the group, scrutinising them all with his sharp eyes. Annabel ran forward, eager to show off. She flew brilliantly from the tree-tops back to the roof of the castle.

'Excellent Annabel, you can come down now.'

Annabel looked disappointed as she landed on the ground.

'Horst,' Mr Burke waved at him to come forward.

Horst walked a few steps forward clutching his bloating stomach. Suddenly, an enormous gale escaped from his body. It propelled Willy into mid-air and sent Mr Burke and everyone else hurtling backwards smashing against the castle wall.

'Stop!' shouted Mr Burke in vain.

Everyone spluttered because the smell was so disgusting. Bridget didn't mind the stench at all and she ran over to help Molly stand up.

'Horst, fly down at once facing us please!' Mr Burke ordered.

Horst had also blasted a hole in one of the trees and its branches hung down forlornly.

'Horst, Go into the barn and sit down,' said Mr Burke, looking at his watch anxiously.

Werner looked as if he wasn't really interested in flying and Mr Burke fidgeted with his tie just as his phone rang.

It was obvious from the conversation that he'd been called to the Professor's office.

'Okay everyone, the rest of you will get some practice tomorrow. Class has ended.' Clearly, he was most unhappy with the group because he mumbled, 'rubbish, loser vampires,' under his breath as he stalked off.

'That's not very nice, Sir. What you're saying hurts our feelings,' Molly chided.

Mr Burke turned around and glared at Molly with contempt. 'Feelings! You're a vampire for heaven's sake. You don't *have* feelings!' Then he sulked off, grumbling to himself.

Molly watched as he left and her face brightened. 'Brilliant luck, class has ended early. Let's have a chat.'

Annabel came closer to Bridget and asked, 'I'm curious. How do you feel?'

Bridget chuckled. 'Actually I feel completely different than normal because I don't *feel* anything. It's really weird. But how come you can smell?' Bridget asked Annabel.

Annabel bristled. 'We're not the norm, most vampires can't smell.'

'Her nickname on the outside is 'Granabel' because she wears false teeth,' said Molly laughing.

Willy giggled but Annabel glared with embarrassment. 'I'm getting my new teeth fitted in a few weeks, you know.'

Bridget smiled warmly and sat up. 'But you do feel thirst for blood, yeah?'

They all nodded. 'Most def. That's one of the few things we have in common with the others,' said Willy.

Bridget laughed. 'But how can you really be un-dead if Horst can feel his farts and Molly can feel her twitching.'

'Bridget, isn't it obvious that we're different? Mallow is the last resort for us. We're outcasts – not pure vampires. We were told to go to hell or to Mallow. The teachers are trying to straighten us out,' said Molly.

'They're not having much luck,' Willy guffawed.

'Annabel has the strongest instincts,' said Molly.

'Can you cry?' Bridget asked Molly.

Molly looked sad. 'No, that's one of the things I miss the most about being human. I'd be nice to cry once in a while.'

Willy patted Molly's sleeve. 'Bridget, Molly is a wannabe-werewolf. She'd love to have what you have.'

'Shhh, Willy. If the Professor heard you say that, he'd kill me on the spot,' Molly said through clenched teeth.

Bridget giggled. 'And I'm a wannabe-vampire. Maybe we can swap.' They all began to laugh loudly.

'And what kills you?' asked Bridget, her eyes sparkling.

Molly flinched. 'We don't like to talk about that but there are only two things: fire and the anti-bodies in a werewolf's saliva.'

Bridget snorted. 'What about a stake to the heart?'

Willy chuckled. 'We don't have hearts.'

Molly waved over at a short blonde vampire. 'That's Suzy. She's afraid of the dark.'

Bridget roared with laughter. 'It's not funny,' said Molly. 'Suzy believes in the boody man.'

Bridget saw that, in their own way, each of the vampires was as compromised as the werewolves. Vampire losers. They were different though, cooler, not remotely animalistic and definitely less emotional. Suddenly Bridget remembered Leona. How could she have forgotten? 'Oh my goodness, do you mind if I have a quick look around for the cup? Where are your bins?'

'You know Bridget, we have already checked the bins but if you insist...' Molly said leading Bridget to the back of the school.

Bridget ran over to some large dustbins, but found to her extreme disappointment they were full of empty *Blud* bottles. She needed to be sure so she rummaged around in the bins for a while. 'No, I don't see anything in here but *Blud*. That's such a pity,' Bridget said clicking her tongue.

'Come on, we've got killing instinct next,' said Molly tugging at Bridget's sleeve.

The Professor welcomed Bridget coldly as she came into the class. 'Tell us again Annabel, how do you feel when you kill?' he said.

Annabel's green eyes sparkled. 'Oh Professor, I feel amazing. It's like a channel of energy runs through my body and gives me life again.' Then Annabel's face registered disappointment and her shoulders slumped. 'Of course with no teeth, I'm missing all the fun.'

'Molly, what's your experience?' asked the Professor.

Molly's body twitched, 'Oh, I'm so hyperactive that I'm biting at prey then moving onto new prey without really appreciating what I'm eating.'

Horst lowered his head. 'My flatulence keeps giving me away just when I'm about to attack my prey, I announce my presence. Sometimes I kill my prey with an über fart. I must find a sol-u-tion.'

Willy yawned into his hand and said, 'Yo Professor, with my low blood count, I'm very weak these days. The only thing I enjoy doing is sitting down with my blaster.'

The Professor sniffed and looked at his watch. 'We've decided to have a new initiative in the school. We're going to run a bat fostering programme.'

Bridget had never heard of anything so crazy. She looked over at Molly who was tapping the legs of her seat over and over with her feet. Molly simply shrugged her shoulders.

'Bats are our dearest friends and when we heard about the explosion in the Mallow caves a couple of days ago, we made some enquiries. Many of the bats died, but we were able to rescue some. Because of the traumatic state in which we found them, we've decided to give them a home here at Dracul's.'

No one spoke.

'I see you're all a little surprised by this. Of course, we've had bats in the castle for centuries but this is different. The idea is that you will each foster a bat. You will look after your bat for the whole term and then when you leave, you can either bring your bat home with you or leave it to be cared for by next term's students.'

Molly put her hand up, 'so they'll be like our pets? We'll mind them while we're here?'

'Precisely Molly. This programme will help you with your rehabilitation and of course you'll be helping another creature as well. It's a win-win situation. You will feed your bats and wash them.' Bridget watched as the Professor's hard face and cold demeanour softened. He chuckled. 'These bats will work here as cleaners getting rid of cobwebs and as security guards alerting us when humans arrive. Beattie, our head bat, has already started the training.'

The window flew open wide and a swarm of baby bats entered the room hovering behind the Professor's head in mid air. The Professor addressed the largest bat, 'Beattie, can you introduce the new bats please?'

'Certainly Professor,' squeaked Beattie, 'we have Barry, Benny, Benji, Bertie, Betty, Breffni, Brenda and...er... Judy.'

'Judy,' repeated the Professor looking straight at the tiny shivering bat.

Judy squeaked. 'I can't pronounce the second letter of the alpha-b-b-bet. I can never say my name during the roll call.' She looked very cute and vulnerable with her hairy black face and tiny wings.

If Bridget wasn't already dead, she thought she would die laughing but she managed to keep the giggles to herself.

'I'll foster Judy,' shouted Molly so spontaneously that tears came to little Judy's eyes.

'Excellent Molly, beamed the Professor. 'Judy, meet your new sponsor.'

Judy flew over to Molly's desk landing on the ink well. Molly and Judy smiled at each other and Judy flew up to Molly's face to give her a tiny kiss.

'She's adorable,' Bridget cooed at her and Judy kissed Bridget's face too but Bridget couldn't feel the tiny feet touching her skin.

'Okay, to get the ball rolling,' said the Professor, 'why don't all the bats fly on to your desks and you can have a chat. See what you have in common and then make a decision about who to foster.'

Soon, the baby bats were chirping away on the various desks and by the end of the lesson, each student had fostered a bat.

***

'How do you like our school?' Willy asked Bridget as they walked towards the dormitory to wake up Vlad.

'It's brilliant. Those baby bats are so cute. I'll be really sorry to say goodbye to Judy.' Bridget continued to feel numb but she was getting used to it by now. They walked up the corridor and Bridget heard a soft cooing sound.

Molly grinned. 'The baby bats have been set up in a nursery. Let's go and have a look.'

Willy didn't appear interested in the bats. Instead he ran ahead to see Vlad.

Molly, Annabel and Bridget walked into a little room with a large white cot in a darkened corner. Bridget rushed over to eight or so bats sleeping on top of a starched white mattress, snoring gently. They were covered in a fluffy white blanket and they all wore tiny white woollen hats. Their little hairy chests rose and fell as they inhaled. A name plaque for each one hung over their heads.

'They are utterly lovely,' said Bridget looking down on them. 'But I thought bats hung upside down?'

'They do,' said Molly pointing overhead to a long rail. 'But they seem to like sleeping in the cot, don't they?'

Bridget looked around and saw a tiny bath and some white towels. She saw a sink and a glass fronted fridge. 'I wonder what's in there?' she asked.

Molly read the top of the tub. 'This must be their food. They eat either dead flies...or dead spiders.'

Bridget noticed something out of the corner of her eye, on the floor under the bat's fridge. It looked like a piece of a large coffee cup. She rushed over and lifted the fridge off the floor.

'You don't think..?' said Molly.

'Does anyone else drink coffee around here?' asked Bridget.

'No.'

'Get me a stick and a plastic bag.'

Molly looked around the room and noticed some plastic on the bat's food tub and then she saw a spatula on top of it.

Bridget grabbed the plastic and lifted the torn cup up with the spatula. 'CSI Mallow,' Molly joked.

'There's very little of it left. What's it smell like?' Bridget asked as she pushed it under Molly's nose.

Molly took a sniff, 'not coffee, it's something sweeter.'

Bridget's voice trembled. 'Hot chocolate. Molly, this could be the cup that Saori used but how did it get up here?'

Molly looked around at the sleeping bats. 'The bats probably carried it up here. Chocolate is sweet. I hope the bats didn't lick it. The poison would make them sick.'

'Looks like it hasn't been licked. I've got to bring it back to Herr Wolf's. This cup could save Leona.' With shaking hands, Bridget wrapped the cup in the plastic and carefully put it into her pocket.

'Come quickly,' Willy bellowed from the hall. 'You've got to see Vlad now.'

Bridget and Molly ran into the dormitory to find Vlad sitting in the middle of the room. Willy guffawed as Vlad relayed some story to him. Vlad was now wearing a green pointed hat, an emerald green waistcoat with black buttons and black pointy shoes. Jigging from left to right he sang, 'on de banks of my own lovely Lee.'

Bridget and the others burst into hysterical laughter. 'Are you sure this antidote works, Bridget? Vlad seems worse than this morning,' asked Annabel.

Vlad looked over and stopped singing. 'Oh, is it yourselves there, Annabel and Molly? Top of the lunchtime to you. Later, I'll tell you lovely people the story of the fairies coming down to Malla one dark evening in the spring of the year but now I must ready meself for a little dancin'. If you'd care to join me, my dear?'

Winking at Annabel, Vlad danced a jig beside her. Everyone exploded in laughter and tears formed in Bridget's eyes. She looked at Willy, who passed close to Molly and took the clear bottle covertly from her hand. Bridget poured the mixture into the *Blud* and gave it back to Willy.

'Yo, here's something to drink,' said Willy, handing Vlad the bottle.

'Is it that strange *red* whiskey you'd be givin' me?' said Vlad, jigging over to Willy's side.

'Yeah, homey,' replied Willy, his voice quaking a little.

'*Fiddle diddle doe and Fiddle diddle dee, Dracul's the on-ly place for me,*' sang Vlad.

Everyone laughed again, but Molly looked on anxiously as Vlad drank the whole bottle in one go.

'I'm feelin' a little sleepy now. I'll take me rest and see you all for a whiskey and a jig later on.' Then Vlad yawned and collapsed onto the side of a coffin.

15

EDDIE'S BLACKMAIL

'What a relief!' said Annabel looking at Vlad snoring, then she sniffed. 'What's that awful smell?'

Bridget inhaled and got a whiff of dung. She could smell again and the stink was her natural body odour returning, the vamp-form was wearing off. She needed to get back to the Institute that instant.

Willy wrinkled up his nose. 'Bridget, you're going to stink this place up. And then the Professor will find and kill you. Molly and Annabel, you need to bring her down to the river now.'

They raced outside. Bridget wanted to have one last flight before she changed back. Lifting off the ground and flying over the castle, Molly and Annabel followed her lead. She looked down at the bridge but there was no sign of Katy. She looked at her watch - it was only half past twelve.

Suddenly, Bridget felt herself dropping out of the sky and she screamed. Molly and Annabel swooped down and caught her just before she crashed on to the grass.

'That was a close one,' said Bridget laughing. She felt her ribs and throat move and knew the potion had almost worn off. Her skin was returning to its natural freckle-stained colour and her long jagged nails shrank.

'We'll wait with you Bridget, if you like?' said Molly falteringly. She and Annabel watched in amazement at Bridget's transformation back to a human.

'That'd be lovely. Katy should be along shortly.'

'How do you feel now?' asked Annabel.

'Well, I feel. That's the most important thing,' said Bridget laughing.

'You are so lucky, Bridget. You're a human-wolf mix and today you've been a vampire too,' said Molly enviously.

'I hadn't thought of it like that. You're right. I am lucky.' Molly covered her nose and Bridget realised that she and Annabel were finding the smell of the river overwhelming. 'You don't have to wait, you know.'

'You did us a massive favour Bridget. We want to make sure that you're alright and that you get back to the Institute safely,' said Molly firmly.

'Bridget, Bridget, I've been worried outta my mind,' Katy shouted as she rushed towards Bridget.

Bridget's face beamed with excitement and she jumped up and cuddled Katy, 'I wish you could've come with me. The college is amazing. It's such a laugh. And the best bit is that I think I've found Saori's cup. I've got it here in my pocket.' Bridget patted her cardigan and grinned.

Katy looked intensely agitated. 'That's great news,' she said half heartedly.

'Hi Katy,' said Molly. Annabel nodded slowly at Katy, taking her in.

Katy sniffed and grinned. All of a sudden, Eddie, in werewolf form, bounded through the bushes, running towards the group. Springing at Molly and Annabel, he howled, 'Hey bloodsuckers, time to die!'

Bridget screamed and everyone went rigid for a second – a bit of delayed reaction. Bridget recovered and stuck out her leg, tripping Eddie up. Eddie tumbled to the ground but bounced back quickly into the pounce position. He gave Bridget a look of reproach and shouted, 'What's wrong with you? They're vampires. It's our job to kill them.'

Molly and Annabel stood together in an automatic defence position and hissed at Eddie. Katy moved well back. Eddie sprang at Annabel but Annabel was too quick for him. He managed to scratch the end of her trousers as she rose in the air. Molly was already dangling from the highest branch of the tree.

As Eddie crashed back on to the ground, Bridget jumped in front of him. 'Eddie, stand down *now*!'

Eddie stood back up challenging Bridget with his body, his nostrils flaring and his fangs showing. Bridget's blood rushed to her quivering face. She was so afraid but instead of retreating, she stepped forward and attempted to snarl in response. Katy seemed completely stunned and didn't stand beside Bridget to support her.

Molly and Annabel watched from the trees and hissed at Eddie. 'If you harm Bridget, we will kill you,' shouted Annabel.

Eddie looked up at Annabel and then glared at Bridget. Bridget felt his panting breath against her face and watched his yellow eyes narrowing. She knew he could kill her right now if he wanted. He pulled back suddenly. 'You stupid she. Wait until I tell the Principal about your being smuggled into the college and stealing potions from the lab. You're in big trouble now, mate.' Then Eddie sprang backwards across the bridge, back to the Institute.

'Eddie, please wait,' shouted Katy. 'I'll go and talk to him,' she said to Bridget before racing after him.

Molly and Annabel dropped down from the trees with a look of horror on both their faces. 'Are you okay?' Molly asked Bridget. Molly began to extend her hand out to touch Bridget but stopped herself abruptly.

'I'm fine,' panted Bridget. 'I'd better go. If I can't convince Eddie to keep his mouth shut, we're all going to be expelled.'

Molly looked disappointed. 'Thanks so much, Bridget. You've already saved our skins.'

'Cheers and thanks,' said Annabel rubbing at the scratch on her trousers.

As Molly and Annabel made to fly back towards the castle, Molly shouted back, 'Bridget, phone me and let me know how it works out. And don't forget about the cup.'

***

Bridget raced towards Katy and Eddie. As she approached them she could hear Katy pleading. 'Please Eddie, don't tell on Bridget.'

'Come on, be a sport,' said Bridget.

Eddie turned his nasty gaze on Bridget. 'Be a sport!' he mocked, 'What's in it for me if I don't grass you up?'

Bridget looked at Eddie's vile face and she responded sourly. 'What will buy your silence?'

Eddie thought for a minute. 'I want to be your best friend from now on. Where you go, I go.'

Bridget gulped and looked at Katy who was already nodding in agreement.

'All right, you're my best friend,' – the word 'friend' laden with sarcasm. 'Now let's get back to the lab to replace the formula before Mr Boyle discovers what I've done.'

A delighted-looking Eddie ran ahead of Bridget and Katy. Bridget turned to Katy in fury. 'Why did you tell him that I went to help the vampires?'

'I was so worried about you Bridget. I thought you were going to get killed over there. I just couldn't keep it to myself. I'm so sorry because I should've known that with Eddie's temper, he'd probably do something stupid.' Katy started to cry and Bridget immediately felt sorry for her.

'Oh Katy, I'm so sorry. I shouldn't have put you under so much pressure. Of course you were worried. But Eddie is the last person I would've told.'

Katy dabbed her eyes. 'I'm sorry. You're right. I've been a real dummy.'

'Well, do me one more favour now by keeping Eddie off my back for twenty minutes.'

'Where are you going?'

Bridget didn't want to confide in Katy again (just in case) so she raised her index finger to her mouth. The first thing Bridget needed to do was cover the cameras with a cloth because she knew she'd never get away with going into the lab illegally twice in one day. The Principal would be bound to pick her up on the camera. Although as luck would have it, it was lunchtime now and all the teachers (including the Principal) were down on the farm.

But the cameras were high and Bridget couldn't reach them. Exasperated, she looked out the window to see Paddy the Painter leaning one of his long ladders against the wall as he took his lunch break. She had an idea - she'd steal the ladder. On her way back in, she grabbed two towels from the toilet and a few minutes later, Bridget had successfully covered the camera in the hall and lab, put back the formulas and uncovered the cameras again. Phew!

Just as she put back the ladder, her phone beeped. It was a text from Katy. 'Come to the farm now. Problem with Eddie.'

***

As Bridget approached the farm, she could hear Eddie's sneering voice and it grated on her already frazzled nerves. When Eddie saw Bridget coming, he ran up to her and gave her a massive lick on the face. Eww! She felt like hurling.

Katy eyed Eddie coldly. 'Hold up Eddie! Give Bridget a chance. She's been sick all morning.'

Bridget recovered and sat next to Simonetta, taking her cardigan off. 'You feeling better?' asked Simonetta.

Bridget nodded.

'Eddie is very friendly today but why, I wonder? Surely he can't keep up the nice guy image. He will snap at one of us before the day is over,' said Simonetta dolefully.

'Oh come on. Let's give him a chance. Maybe this leopard *can* change his spots,' said Bridget nervously.

'I'd really love to see Vlad the Russian again,' said Katy dreamily.

Bridget thought about Vlad for the first time since she'd come back. 'Join the queue, sweetie,' she giggled.

Katy leaned back against the grass, 'I hear that half the she-wolves are in love with him. I wonder what he's doing now?'

Bridget thought about Vlad dancing jigs in his leprechaun garb and she giggled again. This time, Katy joined in.

Eddie looked over as the she-wolves laughed. 'Hey shes, come over here?'

Roald, Dev, Andrew and Miguel all contracted their leg muscles in an aggressive reflex. Bridget thought that they'd better make the effort with Eddie so she stood up. Simonetta whispered to Bridget, 'I'm not sitting beside him, please.'

Simonetta tried to push Bridget ahead of her but Eddie saw that and insisted, 'Oh Simonetta mate, please sit here,' he said, patting the ground beside him.

Roald clenched his fists. Eddie looked around, appearing to enjoy the response he was getting. Bridget and Katy eyed each other nervously and Andrew said, 'Katy and Bridget, why don't you sit next to Roald?'

As Simonetta sat down beside Eddie, Roald's eyes flashed, he opened his mouth to expose dazzling white teeth and his long pointed tongue. Bridget and Katy slumped down beside him and Bridget gave him an affectionate rub which seemed to placate him because his breathing calmed down a little.

Eddie didn't seem to be able to resist pushing the boundaries further. 'Simonetta, have I ever told you how beautiful you are?' he said, nuzzling her shoulder in a provocative gesture.

Roald instantly stood up, rearing his large head and roaring with a mouthful of ferocious teeth. Bridget knew Roald was in danger of shape shifting any second because his eye colour changed from green to gold and she and Katy were flung back by the swift movement of his body.

Andrew jumped in front of Roald, pleading, 'Calm down, Roald, you know what Eddie's like. He's only joking with you.'

Katy moved out of the way.

Roald snapped his head back. 'He is not joking. He is trying to incite me, the Alpha male of this group, isn't he?'

All of them looked at one another in bewilderment. No one had realised that Roald was the Alpha male. They were hardly a pack in the true sense of the word. Their food was supplied so there hadn't been any need for a natural leader to emerge.

Eddie taunted, 'You see, mates. He's arrogant as well as Dutch!'

With outstretched hands, Roald rushed at Eddie. Bridget jumped up to grab Roald's arm in an attempt to stop him.

'Stop it now,' spluttered Bridget. 'There is no Alpha here, er, just a group of friends.'

'Friends, friends!' roared Roald. 'Eddie's not a friend of mine! He's an enemy and I'm going to rip his head off right now!'

Principal Goode and Mr Chow had been walking in the garden. They hurried through the trees when they heard the growls and raised voices. The Principal glared at Roald and Eddie. 'All right everyone, that's enough! Get back to class now.'

Roald continued to snarl at Eddie. Eddie laughed back just as the howl sounded and Eddie mocked. 'Saved by the howl! But don't you worry, we'll get another chance to fight. Mate.'

Roald backed up, his chest heaving and Simonetta rushed over to his side. The tension was electric. Bridget realised that she was in an impossible situation – if she didn't keep the peace, Eddie would reveal everything!

'I think it would be prudent for Eddie and Roald to remain separated today,' said the Principal sharply.

Bridget moved over to Eddie's side and to everyone's obvious surprise said, 'I'll look after Eddie, Principal.'

Roald looked stung by Bridget's suggestion. Andrew, Miguel and Dev watched helplessly, seeming dumbfounded by it all.

The Principal ran her fingers through her fur in agitation. 'Roald, I'll ask Lou to bring you down to the lake to cool off.'

Simonetta gave Roald a pat and he sloped off unwillingly after the Principal and Mr Chow. Katy walked back over to Bridget, looking extremely disappointed.

Eddie walked ahead of Bridget and Simonetta came up behind her, protesting loudly. 'What's going on, Bridget? Eddie is not your friend. It's Roald. I don't understand it.'

Bridget felt conflicted as she stroked Simonetta's shoulder. 'I'm just trying to calm everything down.'

'We'll see you in class, Simonetta. Don't worry, it will all work out, sweet pie!' drawled Katy.

Once Simonetta was out of earshot, Bridget turned to Katy anxiously. 'We can't keep this up. Eddie is pushing us to the limit. Someone could've been killed just now. I think I'll have to tell the Principal everything.'

'No, Bridget,' said Katy in a stern voice. 'I think we should wait.'

Bridget and Katy walked into the Nail Clinic where they saw Eddie with his left arm around Andrew's shoulder. Andrew was far too polite to shrug him off. Bridget and Eddie's eyes met and Bridget looked away quickly.

Eddie raised his paw but continued to look directly at Bridget as he spoke. 'Miss Joyce, can I be excused?'

'All right, Eddie,' Miss Joyce said impatiently.

As he left the class, Eddie winked at Bridget, taunting her further. Once he had closed the door, Bridget stood up nervously and said, 'Miss Joyce, may I please be excused?'

'Really. What is it with you all today? Did you have too much water with your lunch? Oh, go on then.'

Bridget rushed down the corridor towards the Principal's office, to find Eddie waiting outside.

'Oh, I see now, you little toad. Can't be trusted...' said Bridget indignantly.

Eddie sneered at her, wrinkling his nose. 'I can't be trusted. Don't make me laugh! You're the one who broke all the rules. Remember?'

'Are you always this nasty, Eddie? Is this really the kind of person you are?' asked Bridget in dismay.

'I'm just being a model student and reporting a serious indiscretion to the Principal.'

'Not if I get there first,' said Bridget, opening the Principal's door and rushing through it.

The Principal and Mr Chow were drinking tea and chatting and they looked up in shock as Bridget and Eddie stormed into the room together.

'She stole the formula and sneaked into the College!'

'I helped the vampires!'

Bridget and Eddie shouted together, banging their heads in the confusion.

The Principal seethed in her chair when she heard what Eddie said. She ordered both of them to sit down while Mr Chow tried to calm her down. To the extreme anger of the Principal and Eddie, Mr Chow insisted that Bridget tell her story first. Bridget didn't mention that she'd taken the vamp form because she knew this would land her in far more trouble.

After Bridget had finished, the Principal glared menacingly at her. 'But how did you get into the College? Didn't they smell you?' she asked angrily.

'Horst smells really bad. I think he may have masked my smell. And anyway, I didn't go inside.' Bridget knew she wasn't really persuading the Principal.

'Hmmm,' the Principal said not looking at all convinced. Eddie tapped his feet anxiously on the floor, eager to talk and when he did he told everything from the most negative possible point of view, accusing Bridget of treason and treachery. The Principal scowled at Bridget scornfully throughout Eddie's report. And Eddie, well he couldn't wipe the nasty grin off his face.

Mr Chow smiled nervously. 'Principal, I do see this as a positive thing. We have tried over the last few weeks to bring werewolves and vampires together and that is precisely what is happening. We are facilitating cooperation and mutual respect between the two sides. This is just the sort of unstructured affiliation that I was hoping for.'

'Yes, yes, Mr Chow,' replied the Principal, anger creeping into her voice, 'but Bridget has broken rules. And she could've been killed. As a matter of fact, I think Bridget should be expelled.'

Bridget gasped. She didn't want to be expelled and then she remembered. 'The vampires found a piece of the coffee cup. I have it here in my cardigan...' Bridget frowned in dismay when she realised that she'd left her cardigan outside on the grass. 'It's down on the farm. I'll run down now to get it, if you like?'

The Principal shot Bridget a filthy look and shouted. 'You'll go nowhere! Very convenient for the vampires to find the cup on the same day that you visited.'

'It wasn't like that,' said Bridget in an agitated voice.

Mr Chow braided his tentacles again and stared at the Principal, 'I don't think that Bridget should be expelled.'

'But there must be rules, Mr Chow. It's all fine to talk about cooperation but it needs to be supervised, as killings can occur instantaneously. We've already lost Saori, we can't lose another pupil. The programme you've been suggesting is planned, organised and supervised. This,' she gestured towards Bridget, 'was subversive and dangerous!'

'Good point about the supervision – but can't you see, it is going in the right direction?' Mr Chow patted the side of his tea cup with his right tentacle.

The Principal stared out the window, looking furious. After a few moments, she cleared her throat and said, 'Hmmm, yes.' Then she narrowed her eyes and looked callously at Bridget again, her trembling voice betraying the fury that she was suppressing. 'It seems you won't be expelled on this occasion Bridget but watch your step because from now on, I'll be watching you carefully.'

Bridget exhaled, she was hugely relieved. She looked over at Eddie's now savage face. He jumped up and stamped his foot on the floor. 'Whaddya mean letting her off the hook?' Eddie almost took the door off its hinges when he slammed the door behind him.

The Principal looked sternly at Bridget again. 'No more unauthorised meetings with the vampires, is that clear?'

Bridget nodded impatiently.

'And now onto the other important matter. The cup. I'll phone Mr Boyle and tell him you may have the coffee cup from the quiz night. Run down to the farm immediately and get it.'

Bridget jumped up from her seat and hurried outside. Running as fast as she could, she arrived quickly to the spot where she'd taken her cardigan off. But the cardigan was gone. She screamed into her hands in frustration but then realised that one of the others must have taken it back to her room. She ran back up to the classroom and interrupted the lesson asking everyone if they'd seen the cardigan but no one knew where it was. She searched in the dormitory and couldn't find it there either. When she heard Mr Boyle calling her over the intercom, she went down to the lab.

'What do you mean you can't find the cardigan?' shouted Mr Boyle in outrage.

Bridget had never seen him so angry before and it shocked her. 'I'm sorry, so sorry but, but I've asked everyone and searched everywhere and no one has seen it.' Bridget felt like crying and Mr Boyle clearly saw that.

'I was so hopeful that this was the breakthrough that we've been waiting for. But perhaps this cup isn't the one that Saori drank from anyway. There's no way of knowing now. Keep looking for it but if it doesn't show up, we'll simply have to forget about it.'

16

POKE AEROBICS

When Bridget made her way into the common room later that evening, Mr Chow was waiting for her. 'Bridget, the Principal and I would like to discuss something with you.'

Bridget followed Mr Chow down the long corridor to the Principal's office, a knot in her stomach, fearful of what to expect. Perhaps they'd changed their minds and were going to expel her after all. The Principal didn't seem at all happy to see Bridget and she silently indicated for Bridget to sit down. Bridget gulped.

'Bridget, we know you're disappointed about losing the cardigan. We do have an idea that might cheer you up though,' said Mr Chow gently.

Bridget nodded and moved her eyes nervously from Mr Chow to the Principal.

'We have decided to organise another social event between the Institute and the college. And as you seem to be popular among both werewolves and vampires, we'd like you to act as captain again.'

Relief washed over Bridget but she fought not to show it because the Principal was shifting in her seat, frowning. It was obvious she didn't agree with anything that Mr Chow said.

'We want you to captain the Institute team for the Poke Aerobics championships.'

'Poke Aerobics! What's that?' asked a puzzled Bridget.

Mr Chow chuckled, swivelling his eye 360 degrees. 'Bridget, I thought with your knowledge of books and the internet that you'd know all about this. It's only the most popular competitive activity in China. The competing teams poke each other and the first participant to withdraw loses. It's a bit like boxing except that contenders poke instead of punch.'

'I've just ordered overnight delivery of recordings from the final of the Poke Aerobics Championship in Shanghai. It means you'll all have plenty of time to study the rules. I've already phoned the Professor to let him know.' Mr Chow pointed his tentacles at the Principal. 'This Sunday evening does suit us, doesn't it?'

'Yes,' said the Principal curtly.

Bridget got up and ran down the corridor. She decided to phone Molly first to tell her about everything. She'd taken so many risks today - changing into a vampire, going into the college, attending their zany classes, helping Vlad with his leprechaunitis, finding the cup, the row with Eddie, the Principal wanting to expel her and now the Poke Aerobics. She still couldn't believe it had all happened! She knew she could never tell Katy about taking the vamp form. But Molly, Annabel and Willy would keep her secret. And now they had the Poke Aerobics Championships to look forward to. Bridget grinned with delight.

***

Bridget came out of her 'Embrace Your Inner Wolf' class in floods of tears. Lou had finally got her to talk about the death of her father. Crying in front of Lou was humiliating but she couldn't help herself. Lou said that the death of her father had directly affected her feelings about being a wolf. But Bridget had never been that keen on werewolf-dom. She remembered lots of conversations with her surprisingly sympathetic Dad. How she missed him.

Bridget wiped at the tears running down her face and forced herself to think of something else. In a few hours, she'd get to see the vampires again and that made her happy. Down the corridor, she spotted Simonetta carrying a box of bunting.

'I'm putting this on the walls in the sports hall,' Simonetta shouted to her.

Katy ran up behind Bridget. 'Come on, we've got our last practice in the hall.'

Bridget and Katy ran past the study, stopped and looked in. Andrew was typing on the computer. 'Come on, Andrew we're late,' Bridget shouted to him. Dev and Miguel were sitting on a couple of bean bags chatting and they jumped up and followed Andrew out of the room.

Andrew pointed to his MC player. 'Bridget, give me a chance. I've been downloading tracks from Howl Sounds all day.'

'Music is one thing, Andrew, but beating vampires is more important,' said Bridget laughing. 'How does everyone like their track suits?'

'They're plain navy, Bridget. Hardly worth shouting about,' said Andrew.

Dev and Miguel started to run and almost knocked Katy down in the corridor. 'Calm down guys,' shouted Katy, 'no need to push.'

'We're so late,' shouted Miguel and Dev together.

Eddie came around the corner looking jealously at them all. Over the previous few days, relations between him and his classmates had reached an all-time low. He'd been told that he couldn't participate in the Poke Aerobics because of his temper.

Everyone ran gasping into the hall, causing the large swivel doors to bang behind them. Mr Looney looked up and pointed at his watch. They were ten minutes late for their last practice. Mr Looney cleared his throat. 'Okay, then, let's get started. Break into pairs, please.' He noticed Eddie standing, watching. Pointing at some chairs, Mr Looney ordered. 'Eddie, can you move that furniture over there up on to the stage please?'

Eddie looked angrily at the table and chairs but cursing under his breath, he was soon heaving the heavy furniture onto the stage.

'As with the other practices, please choose a partner with whom you've never worked before.'

Bridget had been about to pair up with Katy again because she loved working with her but she chose Andrew instead. He was only a little taller than her so technically it should work. Roald and Dev almost always paired together too so this time Roald chose Katy and Dev chose Miguel.

'Okay. Let's start with Bridget and Andrew then,' said Mr Looney.

Bridget and Andrew walked to the centre of the floor and stood opposite each other, raising their hands. The familiar strains of Mozart's 'Papagayo' began. The violin and staccato notes worked perfectly with the Poke Aerobics rules. The tenor and the soprano both sang their notes separately at first, then in harmony. The sequence was mimicked by the contestants.

'Pa..pa..pa,' sang the tenor. At the same time, Andrew poked Bridget three times in the chest. Then it was the soprano's turn to sing the same three notes, 'Pa, pa, pa,' and Bridget poked Andrew just under his right rib and he started to laugh. The others laughed too, impatient to get their turn.

'No laughing please,' shouted Mr Looney.

Bridget and Andrew continued circling each other with huge grins on their faces. This sport was the most fun Bridget had ever had in her life.

Then the harmony between the tenor and the soprano started and Bridget and Andrew were allowed to poke each other at the same time. Bridget jabbed at Andrew but Andrew was far too quick for her and he jumped sideways, landing a quick poke between Bridget's left lower ribs. She erupted into laughter and staggered a little with the effort of avoiding his second poke. She'd sharpened her nails earlier so even though her pokes tickled, she hoped that they would also hurt. But Andrew had a little belly to insulate him, so he simply laughed when Bridget poked him twice. They continued for a couple of minutes until Andrew poked Bridget three times in quick succession. Suddenly, Bridget lost her balance and landed on her backside on the floor, rolling around in peals of laughter shouting, 'Okay, stop, enough. You win.' Andrew raised his chest in pride and smiled at the others.

Mr Looney strode over and helped Bridget to her feet. 'Let's take a quick break so that I can explain the correct strategy to everyone,' said Mr Looney. 'We've only got two hours to go.'

***

Two utilities engineers (and part time werewolves) chatted happily near the entrance to the Institute. They were attempting to repair the water pipes quickly because Principal Goode wanted this problem rectified before the start of the tournament.

Inside in the assembly hall, Eddie ran out of the visitors' dressing room and grinned when he saw the players coming into the hall. Everyone looked at him uneasily but only Katy spoke to him. 'Hey Eddie, you looking forward to chatting to the Russian about football?'

Eddie frowned. 'No, couldn't care less about him.'

Bridget and Katy chuckled. 'Well, I'm looking forward to seeing him even if you're not,' Bridget said.

Bridget nudged Katy in the ribs. 'Cut it out,' said Katy, 'my ribs are real sore from all the poking.'

The Principal, Lou Flanagan, Penny Lopey, Mr Boyle and Mr Chow came into the hall and Eddie glared at Mr Chow.

Mr Looney was already there, fiddling with his electronic scoreboard for the last time. 'I've set up some drinks there, team. Just take it easy now, few deep breaths and all that,' he said.

The Principal saw the vampires fly by the window and she rolled her eyes. 'Oh, they're here already. Mr Chow, would you care to join me in welcoming them to the Institute,' she said sarcastically.

Within minutes, the whole party returned, including all the students from the college. The Professor, Mr Burke, Penny Lopey and Nano followed behind. Judy and the other baby bats flew overhead. Bridget squinted when she saw that the bats were wearing tiny tracksuits and little white sneakers on their feet. They looked adorable. Bridget waved at Judy bat but ignored Nano's loud complaints about the awful smell in the corridors.

Bridget was more interested in what Molly and the other vampires had on - black-and-yellow tracksuits with the word 'Dracul's' emblazoned across the chest. So cool!

The two teams looked at each and grinned. Bridget, Katy and Andrew approached Vlad, Willy and Molly and extended their hands in welcome.

'Hey Molly,' said Bridget. 'You get my unauthorised text earlier?'

'Yeah! I'm SO excited about this. How's your team doing?'

Bridget screwed up her face. 'I'm a bit useless but the others are pretty good.'

Katy stood back and Annabel came in the door and strode over to her. 'Hello Katy, so nice to meet you again.'

Katy grinned and extended her hand. 'I just love your English accent. I'm doing fine, sweet pie. And how are y'all doing?'

'I'm very well, thank you,' replied Annabel stiffly.

Eddie came over to Katy and ushered her over to the side quite near where Vlad had just sat down. Vlad smiled up at them but they completely ignored him. Roald, Dev and Miguel hung back a little but nodded at Horst. They could see he was wearing some sort of device under his track suit.

Willy rushed over to Bridget. 'Who's in da house? NYC in da house!' and everyone giggled.

'Let's get started,' said the Principal who was standing on the podium with an uncomfortable smile on her face.

The teams separated, one to each side of the hall. 'First up, we would like to welcome you all here to the Institute tonight. The rules are simple. Each contestant must attempt to poke his opponent. When one of the opponents falls, the opposing team member is considered the winner. To start, we have Bridget from Herr Wolf's Institute against Molly from Dracul's College.'

Bridget and Molly moved to the centre of the hall and faced each other. They kept serious faces (it was meant to be a competition, after all). Mr Looney looked at his scoreboard and announced, 'When the buzzer sounds, you have three minutes in which to Poke each other. If after three minutes, there is no clear winner, we will move on to the next participants from both schools.'

The buzzer sounded, the violins at the beginning of 'Papagayo' started and a big cheer went up. Bridget attempted to poke Molly but Molly was far too quick and Bridget wasn't able to make contact with her at all. Molly took advantage of this by poking Bridget several times in the side.

Bridget squirmed and burst out laughing. She was still trying desperately to poke Molly but wasn't having much luck. Molly ducked when Bridget tried to poke her and on the rebound Molly poked Bridget over and over to the point where Bridget yelled in hysterics, 'Stop, stop, I give up.'

Molly grinned and turned to look at the cheering vampires behind her. The scoreboard changed to show Dracul's leading by one point.

The next contestants were Willy and Roald. The music started again and they circled each other with their hands raised, ready to jab out at any moment. Roald got a poke in first and it made Willy wobble slightly. Willy gulped and started again. Roald was managing to poke Willy furiously but every time Willy's body shook, his face got paler and paler. It was obvious from the way he stumbled that he was close to fainting. Roald saw this as an opportunity to inflict more discomfort and he started to hold Willy with one arm while he poked him with the other.

Willy chuckled after every poke and tried in vain to loosen the grip on him but Roald was physically much stronger. Roald was the clear winner and he looked up at the scoreboard to see two seconds remained. From the sidelines, everyone cheered and screamed. Just as the bell sounded, Willy fainted.

The Professor looked on, irritated and instructed Mr Burke to carry Willy over to the side next to a snoring Vlad.

'Let's have a break in play,' said the Principal. 'The score is Herr Wolf's one, Dracul's one. We've set up your drinks in the locker room over there,' she said dismissively to the vampires, pointing to the back of the hall.

17

THE FIRE

Annabel, Molly, Suzy and Werner grouped together and walked towards the changing rooms. Horst ran into the corridor, looking for the toilet and Andrew rushed after him.

Katy hurried over to Bridget anxiously. 'Annabel left her bottle of *Blud* here. I need to powder my nose, honey. Can you give it to her?'

Bridget nodded and strode over to the changing room, delighted at the chance of having a quiet chat with the vampires.

As the vampires opened the door, Eddie pointed to the back of the room and said. 'I've left your drinks in the cabinet there.' Bridget walked up behind them.

'Oh, thanks,' said Molly. Turning to Annabel, she whispered, 'he's changed his tune. He wanted to kill us the other day.'

'Here Annabel, you left your *Blud* outside,' Bridget said.

'Where did you say you put the drinks?' asked Molly, turning in time to see Eddie close the door.

Bridget heard the lock turn and she flinched. 'That's funny. It smells like smoke in here. Any of you been smoking?' she asked nervously.

'You must be joking, Bridget. Fire kills us. Only a vampire with a death wish would ever smoke a cigarette,' said Molly ruefully.

Within a few seconds though, Bridget knew that she hadn't imagined the smell and she inhaled deeply. 'Something's burning in here,' she said tensely.

The vampires shrieked in terror. Bridget looked beyond the lockers and her heart sank. Smoke curled out and she could see small flames lighting the walls. 'Come on, let's get out of here!' she shouted.

Everyone ran to the doors, but they wouldn't open. 'They're locked,' shouted Molly in horror.

Bridget shoved Molly aside, 'they can't be, let me try.' Bridget jabbed the door handle up and down. Her stomach lurched. They were locked in.

The smoke inside grew stronger, making it difficult to see in the room. Little fragments of burned paper fluttered up to the ceiling. Annabel, Molly and Suzy screamed for help and banged on the door and Werner began to cough loudly.

A small plume of smoke curled out through the grids of the extractor fan over the doors. 'There's a fire!' Roald's voice shouted.

Judy flew out of Molly's coat pocket from the coat hook outside and hovered in front of the door. She started to wail, flapping her tiny wings against the doors. The other baby bats swarmed around the extractor fan, looking in and squeaking. Two of them fell to the floor coughing as the smoke blasted out through the grid.

The Principal, Professor and Mr Chow pulled at the door from the outside. Lou Flanagan and Mr Boyle broke the glass on the two fire extinguishers in the hallway and pulled out the hoses. The Principal turned the hose to the on position but no water came out. 'The mains water is still not repaired,' she shrieked.

'Roald, Miguel, Andrew and Dev, try to knock down the door with your bodies!' shouted the Principal.

All four male werewolves stood in front of the door with Roald shouting, 'One, two, three, four, *heave*!' They pushed desperately against the door but although it rattled a little, it remained solid in its hinges.

'Get those axes on the fire alarm,' shouted Bridget from inside. 'You can break it down!'

Vlad and Willy woke up from their sleep and rushed over to help too.

The blaze was getting stronger and Bridget could hardly see in front of her. There was an eerie sound of crackling paper and Bridget began to hack. Annabel, Molly, Werner, and Suzy stood beside Bridget banging their hands repeatedly on the doors. Bridget looked into Molly's terrified eyes. Vampires could feel terror, no doubt about it now. She screamed at Roald through the keyhole. 'You've got to get us out. It's getting worse.'

Roald and Dev grabbed two axes, raised them behind their heads and swung them at the door. The first cut made an impact and the wood in the doors began to splinter, but it was clear that it would take many swings before the doors could be broken down.

Undeterred, Roald and Dev continued with the axes, the sweat pouring off their bodies. Thick smoke came out from under the door and the coughing within the room got worse. The Professor's cool eyes blazed as he watched helplessly and he grabbed Nano's arm for support. Bridget screamed and slammed her body against the door.

'Help us. Help us,' cried Molly through the crack in the door. Judy squeaked and shivered and the other baby bats flew overhead wailing. Dev and Roald had created holes in the wood and were shoving their hands in to push away the wood between the cracks. They could see Bridget and the vampires standing inside the door, shouting. Plumes of black smoke billowed into the hall.

Now that there were two large holes in each door, Bridget pushed her hands out and held on to the doors. Roald looked directly at Bridget's frantic eyes. She coughed at him loudly and he shut his eyes in despair. He and Dev pulled more wood away from the door.

'Help them with the wood,' shouted Bridget. The vampires rushed forward, pulling at the remaining wood and breaking pieces from it. Bridget was almost deaf from the cries for help around her.

Bridget looked back. They were running out of time. Soon she and the vampires would be incinerated. It seemed hopeless. Her tears fell on her cheeks as she struggled to pull off the wood. For the first time, she realised how much she truly loved the vampires. Yes, *loved* them. They weren't perfect, that was why. Their differences no longer mattered - they had proved that they were great friends. She thought of each individual vampire. Her eyes snapped open. 'Horst, Horst, blast the doors with one of your farts. Hurry, Hurry.'

Horst had been standing near the Professor and he shouted with joy. 'Of course . An über fart is what's required. Wűnderbar idea, Bridget. Now move back from the doors, everybody!'

On both sides of the doors, vampires and werewolves moved well back. Horst took position as far away as he could and then turned his back. 'I need to be very precise if I am to hit my target.'

Bridget shouted encouragement to him but her voice was now very hoarse. Putting his hands on his knees, Horst raised his posterior in line with the central lock of the door. Taking a deep breath in and using the muscles of his stomach, he pressed down hard on his intestines. At once, his body jolted forward and a gale of fart hammered the door. The door buckled and some air blasted through the holes in the door but the door did not collapse.

The methane gas that had come into the changing room swirled around, sucking the fire into it. Bridget looked back at the fire as it came closer still. She was crestfallen. Molly and Annabel hugged each other helplessly. Suzy and Werner gasped in terror, their piercing eyes almost blinding Bridget.

Outside, the air from the fart rebounded off the door and blasted everyone. They tumbled to the ground and lay sprawled on the floor, holding their noses.

Mr Chow grasped the Principal, exasperated. 'Why are these doors so strong?'

Suddenly, the Principal seemed to remember something. 'Bridget, the doors have special hinges but they're weaker on the inside. The only way to get you out is if you shape shift now.'

Bridget shook her head and looked at Molly and Annabel. She couldn't cope with the shame of shifting in front of the vampires. It was just too much to ask. Then she looked into Roald and Andrew's pleading eyes. 'Come on, Pidge,' said Andrew sobbing. 'You can do it.'

Bridget began to cry softly and saliva dripped off the corners of her mouth, on to her blackened face.

'Please Bridget,' rasped Molly. 'You're our last hope.'

Judy squeaked, 'Don't let my Mommy die, Bridget.'

Bridget rubbed Molly's hand, her eyes frantic. She had no other choice. 'I might kill you after I shape shift. I'll have no control over myself, you know.'

Molly shuddered. 'We'll have to take that chance.'

'Hurry, hurry,' shouted the Principal angrily as she looked at the flames behind their heads. 'It's not the full moon so one of you will have to provoke Bridget. She can't do it on her own.'

Molly fidgeted with her hands anxiously and Annabel moved in front of her. 'I'll do it.'

'Hit her hard,' the Principal screamed. 'And then stand well back.'

Bridget looked terrified as Annabel raised her left hand to strike her. Bridget felt the excruciating pain immediately and she howled. Roald closed his eyes and muttered. The Professor and his staff looked away.

Immediately, Bridget pounced on all fours and thrashed her head from side to side, howling as her eyes changed colour. Annabel and Molly hugged each other closely but they couldn't take their eyes off Bridget. Amid loud groans, Bridget's back curved and her rib cage expanded to three times its size. Her shoulders hunched and she tossed her head back as her tail shot out from her back and her neck lengthened. Her clothes fell off in tatters. Her tongue and powerful teeth snapped as her snout formed. Hair grew quickly over her whole form, covering her body entirely. She looked down to see her feet and hands elongate into paws.

Growling savagely, Bridget turned to face the vampires. She felt her long tongue run across her fangs. It looked like she had some vampires to kill. Molly and Annabel shrieked in horror, clutching at each other.

The Principal and students shouted from outside. 'Bridget, knock the door down!'

Bridget panted and scanned the Principal's eyes. When she looked at the vampires again and saw the fire, she remembered what she was supposed to do. Raising herself up on her hind legs, she slammed her body against the doors which wobbled and shook. 'One more time,' screamed the crowd outside the door. Bridget howled savagely when she struck the door with her body a second time. This time, the doors fell away a little and the grip of the hinges loosened.

Roald and Andrew pulled at the damaged doors and dragged them down. Instantly, Bridget sprang out of the opening.

Molly, Annabel, Suzy, and Werner followed Bridget out, running with their arms raised, their bodies covered in smut. They were quickly enveloped by the arms of their friends, Horst, Willy and Vlad and the werewolves.

Molly shook all over as she fell into Roald's strong arms and she didn't mind it one bit when he licked her hair. Tears streamed down Annabel's face as Horst and Willy hugged her. Judy bat jumped onto Molly's head and used her tiny wings to wipe the dirt from her face.

Andrew cuddled Suzy who found a warm heart beating against her dirty face. Dev patted Werner's shaking body and reassured him. Not one of the vampires resisted the physical comfort. All were happy to be alive.

Bridget watched the display and her temper began to rise. Howling, she paced up and down and her yellow-green eyes flashed. Roald and Andrew disentangled themselves from the vampires and stared anxiously at Bridget.

'She's getting ready to attack,' the Principal said in a frightened voice.

'She won't attack us,' said Andrew and Roald together.

They walked gingerly towards Bridget and smiled at her. Sniffing deeply, Bridget watched as her friends approached. When she recognised their scent, her heart rate slowed down. They weren't a threat to her - she loved them with all her heart.

Andrew ran over and stroked the fur on Bridget's back. Her breathing steadied and she felt calmer.

'Get her a coat,' cried Andrew. 'She needs clothes.'

Everyone waited in silence as Simonetta rushed over and shielded Bridget from their eyes. After a few low groans, Bridget's stumbling and coughing human form, stepped forward towards the waiting group.

Annabel and Molly who were completely covered in soot and ash ran to Bridget first. 'Oh Bridget. You've just saved our lives. Thank you,' Molly said hugging her forcefully. Molly wheezed and Bridget laughed nervously.

Suzy, Werner, Horst and Willy rushed over. 'You've saved us all!' they said, cuddling her.

Roald, Andrew and Miguel jumped up in the air and gave each other high fives. The Principal exhaled and Mr Chow patted her on the shoulder. The Professor and his teachers watched the scene with silent seething eyes.

Just then, Bridget's mum and Paddy the painter rushed into the room. Mary screamed when she saw Bridget surrounded by vampires and she lunged towards Willy in defence. 'Bridget, you're in danger. He's trying to kill you!'

Bridget felt terrified. Tearing herself away from Willy's arms, she jumped in front of her mother and shoved her body away, her hoarse voice swollen with emotion. 'Mum, stop. Willy's not trying to kill me. He's my friend!'

Principal Goode quickly joined in to pacify Mary. 'Mary, it's okay. Willy is her friend. Calm down now.'

Mary looked at Bridget's pleading face in horror. 'But he's a vampire...'

Bridget grabbed her mother to steady her. 'Mum, please believe me. They're my friends. Someone started a fire here. We almost died.'

'Mary, you will be very pleased to know that Bridget shape shifted voluntarily tonight to save her own life and the lives of some of the vampires,' said Mr Chow proudly.

Mary looked stunned. 'Really, Pidge. Is that true?'

Bridget bit her lip and nodded her head.

Andrew shouted, 'three cheers for Bridget.' And the room was full of noise.

Mary took her eyes off Bridget and looked at the broken down doors and all the smoke in the room. The water had finally come back on and Lou and Mr Looney were dousing the fire with the hoses. Mary suddenly remembered why she'd come to the school. 'Where's Katy?'

Bridget looked around. She'd completely forgotten about Katy. 'Where is she?' she asked the others, worry etched on her face.

No one seemed to know. 'I haven't seen her since before the fire started. And actually I haven't seen Eddie either...' said Andrew quizzically.

Mary's face looked strained. 'Katy is trying to kill you, Bridget.'

'What?' Bridget gasped. 'What are you talking about?'

'I found this letter. It's from your father.'

The Principal extended her hand out to Mary. 'Probably best if I read it, Mary.' Mary gave her the letter and the Principal cleared her throat and began to read loudly.

My dearest darling Mary

If you are reading this letter then I am no longer alive. Thinking about you and Bridget living without me just breaks my heart but I know that I must write this letter now, to protect Bridget's life.

Bridget pulled her mother closer to her and groaned.

It will be a shock for you to know this but in my youth, I was a member of the werewolf resistance or WEEsistance. I got involved in all the usual resistance activities like sabotaging werewolf meetings and intercepting messages from the USN.

Bridget stole a look at Mr Chow and saw that he was unusually tense.

Once Bridget was born, I realised that my beliefs could put her life in danger so I decided to give up the cause. I returned to Nashville to tell the local unit there of my decision. My two oldest friends, Steve and Robert, tried to persuade me out of it but I wouldn't let them. My mind was made up.

Two days after I got home to Ireland, I had a phone call from Steve saying that Robert had been killed and that everyone blamed me for his murder. I vowed to return to clear my name but Steve warned me that my life would be in danger if I did. Bridget was so young that I didn't risk returning. But recently I received an anonymous letter from Nashville telling me that Robert's daughter Katy wanted to avenge her Daddy's death. She intended to come to Ireland to kill Bridget.

Bridget screamed in anguish and the Principal looked up. 'This letter is unfinished. Was there more to it, Mary?'

Mary shook her head solemnly. 'No. That was it.'

There was a hushed silence as the students watched. Bridget's shoulders shook and she began to sob loudly. Roald and Andrew moved in and put their hands on her shoulders. All the vampires stared uncomfortably and waited. After a few moments, Bridget began to speak, though it was difficult to understand her. 'But I trusted her, Katy was my best friend.'

Mary held Bridget's face. 'She's twisted, Pidge, just twisted.'

Molly swallowed hard but although she appeared to be trying to control herself, she burst out crying. Annabel moved to her side and began to wail tearlessly. 'We trusted Katy too, Bridget. She fooled us all,' whispered Molly.

Bridget looked at Molly in shock. She was crying with un-wet tears. The Professor sniffed and gave Molly and Annabel a withering look of contempt.

Principal Goode turned to Bridget impatiently, 'How did the fire start?'

'All I know is that it started immediately after Eddie left the locker room. And then we couldn't open the doors.' said Bridget, sniffling.

The Principal nodded. 'It's fairly obvious that Katy and Eddie are responsible.'

She looked over at Mr Chow, whose tentacle arms and legs were waving about, causing him to stagger a bit. 'We will find and punish them,' he said firmly, clearly trying to take control.

'Quickly, everyone. We will pursue them now. There isn't a moment to lose. Lou and I will shape shift and sniff out their scents,' the Principal said walking towards the door. The students made to follow the Principal.

Mr Chow looked at the Professor. 'It would assist greatly if you and your students helped in the hunt too.'

The Professor nodded slowly in agreement, a sneer on his face.

'Come on, Pidge. We need you,' said Andrew, turning back, but Bridget didn't move.

Mary wrapped a protective arm around Bridget. 'She's exhausted. We'll just wait here. Is that okay, darling?'

'Yes,' said Bridget sadly, dabbing her eyes.

'We'll stay with Bridget too,' said Molly looking over at Annabel. 'There are more than enough vampires to help.'

Vlad, Willy, Horst and Werner lined up beside Roald, Andrew, Dev and Miguel: The first ever werewolf vampire hunting party.

'Let's go!' shouted Principal Goode. 'They've got a head start.'

18

RETRIBUTION

Bridget and Mary slowly climbed the stairs to the dormitory. Bridget wanted to have a shower and get some clean clothes. She'd never felt so dreadful in all her life. The stress of the fire and Katy's betrayal was taking its toll on her. Slight bruising was beginning to appear on her body and she used extra shampoo to get rid of the horrible smell of smoke. She sobbed intermittently, as the water washed off her skin.

After Bridget had dried off, she lay on her bed and the tears returned. She replayed the last few weeks in her head. How could she have been so stupid, so fooled? She saw it all now. Katy *had* really tried to kill her in the park at Halloween. And if it hadn't have been for Molly, she would have succeeded. Katy must've poisoned the hot chocolate too and killed Saori by accident. But how could Katy have lied so easily and so often? Had everything been fake, all the laughter, the hugs? Why hadn't Bridget used her animal instinct to sniff out Katy's deceit? But of course, she'd been rejecting her instincts every day. And her Dad really was in the WEEsistance. Is that why the teachers were so interested in her?

'Do you feel like sleeping,' Mary asked looking very concerned.

'No,' sniffled Bridget, looking out the window. 'I need to phone Leona and let her know she's no longer a suspect.'

'You can do that later.'

Bridget looked out again as the dawn light outside began to creep into the room. It was almost morning and she knew they'd have to stop hunting before the humans woke up.

'There's no word yet. But Molly and Annabel will come up when they get back.'

Bridget sobbed into her hay pillow.

All of a sudden, Bridget heard a swishing sound in the corridor and then a sharp rap on the dormitory door. 'Bridget, they're back,' said Molly, her voice hesitant, doleful. 'And Katy and Eddie are with them.'

Bridget shot up in the bed, her heart pounding. 'I don't want to see her,' she cried anxiously.

Mary looked sternly at Bridget. 'You must come down and confront her, Pidge. We need to get this over with.'

Molly looked at Bridget with pleading eyes but said nothing. Bridget inhaled, got up slowly and patted her dress. She knew there was no way around it. She'd have to face up to Katy.

***

As Bridget, Mary and Molly walked into the assembly hall, they saw that the werewolves, vampires and bats had formed a circle.

Bridget's stomach flipped when she heard Katy's voice. 'I told you to put paraffin on the paper,' she was shouting at Eddie.

Bridget swallowed the lump in her throat and everyone turned when they heard her approach. Katy and Eddie were tied up in silver chains. They could never escape those. Katy's hair was unkempt but she continued to snarl and pull against her binding. Her nose twitched involuntarily when she clearly sniffed Bridget's scent but she didn't make eye contact with Bridget.

The Principal and Mr Chow walked over to Bridget, looking triumphant. 'We've caught them,' said the Principal fiercely.

Bridget swallowed again and stared at the former best friend who wouldn't meet her gaze. Only Katy could give Bridget answers and she needed an explanation.

'Why did you do it, Katy?' asked Bridget, her voice trembling. She didn't want to cry although her lips were quivering and she didn't know if she could hold out. The werewolves looked over at Bridget and whispered amongst themselves.

Katy raised her head for the first time and looked Bridget directly in the eye. Her eyes were full of hate. 'You know why I did it,' Katy spat. 'Your father deprived me of my Daddy, all these years. I wasn't going to let you get away with that.'

Bridget felt her despair rising. 'But I did nothing to you at all and my Dad didn't kill your father...'

Mr Chow interrupted Bridget, 'That's quite right. We have proof that Patrick didn't do it. I contacted the USN and they sent me this.' From between his tentacle fingers, he waved a letter at everyone in the room. 'It's a confession from Steve, Katy's step-father to the murder of her real father Robert.'

Katy narrowed her eyes and seethed. 'I don't believe the USN. You lie about everything. You probably forged that letter. I'll never believe that Steve killed my real father.'

Bridget felt shocked at Katy's continued aggression and obvious hatred. 'But it's here in black and white. Can't you see it's the truth?' shouted Bridget, pointing to Mr Chow.

'All I know is that I hate you, Bridget. And I'll never stop hating you.'

A sob erupted from Bridget's mouth and she started to cry again. The young werewolves formed a cluster around her and Molly and Annabel hissed at Katy in defiance. Eddie's usual sneer was gone and his vacant eyes looked utterly defeated. He moved his body away from Katy's.

'It doesn't matter who you believe killed your father, Katy. You have committed a crime, punishable by death,' shouted the Principal impatiently. 'I will kill you myself now.'

'You will do no such thing,' protested the Professor angrily. 'Katy and Eddie tried to kill four vampires as well. I must be involved in their sentence. It is the law. And I can assure you that our methods are far more tortuous than a quick bite to the jugular.' The Professor's piercing eyes taunted the Principal.

Mr Chow sighed and turned to an enraged-looking Principal. 'The Professor is correct. It is the law. We will have to hold a trial with a werewolf and vampire jury. I will take Katy and Eddie back to Geneva now. My soldiers are waiting outside.'

With that, he pressed on a small black calculator strapped to one of his tentacle fingers and ten soldiers, wearing crimson uniforms with black buttons, marched noisily into the room. 'They will be incarcerated in the prison for serious crimes. But you and the Professor will choose the judge and jury.'

The Professor looked over at the Principal condescendingly and her face burned with anger.

'Take these criminals to my plane,' Mr Chow shouted to his soldiers.

As Katy was being marched out of the room, she ducked under the arms of one of the soldiers and made a run for Bridget. Everyone froze as she came closer to the group with her arms outstretched, screaming. Roald shoved Andrew and Annabel out of the way and he placed his body in front of Bridget who was inhaling sharply, feeling like she might choke.

Molly flew down and landed with her feet on Katy's shoulders. Then she spun Katy's body around and around. Katy stumbled and fell to the ground pathetically swiping at Molly. Finally, Molly lowered herself down to face a dizzy Katy. Molly smiled cruelly as she hit Katy square in the face. 'That's for trying to kill Bridget and me.'

Katy bent over and screamed in agony as she clutched her face. Molly opened her mouth and pushed out her fangs.

'Don't bite her,' shouted the Professor. Molly looked at him, turned and stepped back.

The soldiers quickly dragged Katy out of the room. In spite of the pain from Molly's punch, Katy continued to rage and wrestle with them.

Bridget had to sit down, her breathing grew shallower and she suddenly felt very faint. Maybe she should finally accept her werewolf self – it had saved her life tonight after all. She looked around her at all the concerned faces of her friends – a bunch of werewolf and vampire misfits. She truly loved every one of them. Her life had almost ended tonight but she knew, with these friends in tow, a new life was only beginning.

THE END

Glossary of Terms

Alpha Male   *Leader of the wolf pack*

Anaemia   *A deficiency of red blood cells*

Badger Hunt   *A game were-cubs play to develop their running abilities*

Barking Attendants   *Hounds who act as werewolf security*

Bat Fostering   *Temporary parenting of baby bats*

'Blaster   *Ghetto blaster or large music player*

Bovine Tuberculosis   *Bacteria that causes tuberculosis in cattle*

Blud   *Patented drink of bottled blood with varieties 'liet' and 'extra'*

'BORN TO BE WILD'	*Werewolves official anthem*
CIAO	*Hello/Goodbye in Italian*
DA	*Russian word for yes*
DUHALLOW HOUNDS	*Hounds who are members of the oldest hunt in Mallow, Ireland*
DISTEMPER	*A viral disease of animals which causes fever and coughing*
DORAPHOBIA	*The fear of touching animal fur or skin*
DRACUL'S COLLEGE	*Famous rehab for vampires*
EMOTIONAL ROLLERCOASTER	*Fun park ride with thirty eight mood swings*
EYE GOUGERS	*Group that force thumbs into others eyes*

Fade Drops   *Drops that when applied or swallowed cause disappearance*

Fairy Fort   *The home of the leprechaun*

Flowery-col   *Cauliflower backwards: the opposite of brocoli*

Four Brush Technique   *Painting Technique where four brushes are used simultaneously*

Giddy bytes   *Memory found on the computer of a horse*

Herr Wolf's Institute   *Famous rehab for werewolves*

Hola   *Hello in Spanish*

Howlo   *Official werewolf social networking site set up by Bridget*

Hyper-wolf   *An overly aggressive werewolf*

IDIOTIC NEWS	*Radio station and website which features idiotic stories*
INNER WOLF THERAPY	*Deep counselling course for traumatised werewolves*
LEPRECHAUNITIS	*Disease that occurs after leprechaun bite*
LYME DISEASE	*An acute inflammatory disease caused by bacteria in the bite of a deer tick*
MALLOW	*A town in Co Cork, Ireland*
MALLOW CASTLE	*A castle in the town of Mallow*
MANGE	*A skin disease common to wolves*
METAMORPHOSE	*Change from a human to a werewolf*

MID-WOLF *A state somewhere between human and wolf*

MITE INFESTATIONS *Being invaded or overrun by parasites*

MYXOMATOSIS *A viral animal disease (usually fatal)*

NARCOLEPSY *A sleep disorder characterized by sudden and uncontrollable sleep*

OCTT *Out of control territory-marking tendencies*

PAPAGAYO *Meaning bird in German: Famous piece of Mozart music*

PAROVIRUS *Common parasites that live on the fur of wolves*

Pass the Weasel   *A game were cubs play to develop their motor skills*

Poke Aerobics   *A tournament where opponents poke each other*

Privjet   *Hello in Russian*

Raboutin   *Shoes made from rabbit skin*

Red Whiskey   *What a leprechaun calls 'Blud'*

Revamp   *Vampire Rehab*

Scratch Dancing   *A werewolf dance where partners scratch each other*

Severe Flatulence   *Bad case of farting*

Shape shifting   *Process by which a human changes into a werewolf*

SKIN CRAWLERS	*People with severe eczema*
SPOT THE TRAP	*A game were cubs play to develop their visual abilities*
ÜBER FART	*An enormous fart – German origin*
UNITED SUPERNATURAL NATIONS	*Official Organisation for Supernatural Beings*
UN-WET TEARS	*Tears from a Wannabe-Werewolf Vampire*
VADD	*Vampire Attention Deficit Disorder*
VAMPFORM	*A potion that temporarily transforms a werewolf into a vampire*
WUPS	*Werewolf pups*
WERE-CUBS	*Slightly older wups*
WEEHAB	*Werewolf Rehab*

WEESISTANCE	*Official organisation for resisting werewolf identity*
WÜNDERBAR	*The German word for wonderful*
ZEN CHOW	*Head of the United Supernatural Nations*